NARUTO

MISSION: PROTECT THE WATERFALL VILLAGE!

Date: 5/17/16

GRA KISHIMOTO
Kishimoto, Masashi,
Naruto. Mission: protect the
waterfall village! /

NARUTO™
MISSION: PROTECT THE WATERFALL VILLAGE!

Original Concept by
Masashi Kishimoto

Written by
Masatoshi Kusakabe

Translated by
Tomo Kimura with Janet Gilbert

VIZ Media
San Francisco

NARUTO – TAKIGAKURE NO SHITOU OREGA HERO DATTEBAYO!-
© 2003 by Masashi Kishimoto, Masatoshi Kusakabe
All rights reserved.
First published in Japan in 2003 by SHUEISHA Inc., Tokyo.
English translation rights in the United States of America and Canada arranged by SHUEISHA Inc.

© 2002 MASASHI KISHIMOTO

Art by Minako Shiba/Mirei Takioka
Coloring by Emiko Takai
Background art by Kazuko Koyanagi

Cover design by Sam Elzway
All rights reserved.

No portion of this book may be reproduced or transmitted in any form or by any means without written permission from the copyright holders.

Published by
VIZ Media, LLC
295 Bay Street
San Francisco, CA 94133

www. viz.com

Library of Congress Cataloging-in-Publication Data

Kishimoto, Masashi, 1974-
[Naruto. Takigakure no shito, ore ga eiyu datte ba yo. English]
Naruto. Mission: protect the waterfall village! / original concept by Masashi Kishimoto ; written by Masatoshi Kusakabe ; translated by Tomo Kimura with Janet Gilbert.
p. cm.
"First published in Japan in 2003 by Shueisha Inc., Tokyo"--T.p. verso.
ISBN-13: 978-1-4215-1502-1
ISBN-10: 1-4215-1502-4
I. Kusakabe, Masatoshi, 1964- II. Kimura, Tomo. III. Gilbert, Janet. IV. Title.
PL872.5.I57N3713 2007
895.6'36--dc22

2007030004

Printed in the U.S.A.

First printing, October 2007

CONTENTS

PROFILE

MEET SQUAD SEVEN

NARUTO UZUMAKI
A boy with a big dream—and a big secret. The spirit of the demonic Nine-Tailed Fox is sealed deep inside him. Can Naruto still become the best ninja in the land?

SASUKE UCHIHA
The last living member of the prestigious Uchiha clan. A ninja-in-training with skills far beyond his years.

SAKURA HARUNO
Squad Seven's brainy female. She loves bossing Naruto around, but has eyes only for Sasuke.

KAKASHI
Squad Seven's fearless sensei since they graduated from the ninja academy. His signature weapon? The mysterious Sharingan Eye.

THE OTHERS

SHIBUKI
The young, cowardly leader of the remote Hidden Waterfall Village.

SUIEN
A powerful rogue ninja who desperately craves the Hidden Waterfall's most precious possession.

SENJI
An elderly ex-ninja and Shibuki's compassionate aide.

THE BEGINNING

In the middle of a pristine lake, Hisen stood on a tall geyser, rapidly moving his fingers. The leader of the Hidden Waterfall Village had high hopes for the ninjutsu he was about to release. His attackers had been surprisingly tough, and now they were treading water in a circle around him, poised for his next move.

This one should do the job, Hisen thought. He finished his signs, looked up, and shouted at the sky.

"Water Style: Lotus Light Rupture!"

The geyser instantly started to rotate, forming drops of water that looked like lotus petals. It was a lovely sight, like something you might see in a Zen garden. The liquid petals got bigger and bigger, then spun off with explosive energy in every direction.

Hisen's attackers snickered as the petals zoomed toward them. They were already soaking wet. How could even more water hurt them? Suddenly a ninja cried out in agony and sank in a spray of blood. Another ninja was hit, then six or seven more. The liquid lotus petals were not as delicate as they looked: Hisen's chakra had transformed them into razor-sharp killing machines.

A few ninja escaped the attack by sliding backward on the lake's surface, but the watery weapons they thought they had dodged soon hit them from behind. Minutes later, every ninja was gone. Only their leader was still alive, a man in a red mask.

"You're still standing? But that was my best jutsu!" Hisen cried, pale and gasping for breath. He was reaching his physical limit.

The masked man stood on the now-placid lake, arms folded across his chest. He stared at Hisen long and hard before he finally opened his mouth.

"Now I see the real power of the Hero's Water," he sneered. "You're almost done for, old man." He threw back his head and had a good laugh.

Then he quickly slid toward Hisen, throwing a shuriken with one hand and making a sign with the other. Hisen tried to avoid the attack, but his chakra was waning fast. He slowly started sinking into the water.

"Die! Fire Style: Flame Screen Gale!" the masked man shouted, spitting out a flaming tornado.

The Fire Style Jutsu, which could incinerate anything it touched, sizzled when it hit the water. Hisen disappeared behind a dense cloud of steam. The masked man laughed again, sure of his victory.

"Ha! My jutsu makes everything burn like paper! Die, Hisen of Hidden Waterfall!" he shouted gleefully.

When the wind blew the steam away, Hisen was nowhere to be seen. The only thing left was his jacket, now burning to a crisp on the water. Hisen had appeared to be completely out of chakra. But was he?

"Where...where'd he go?" the masked man choked, looking around desperately.

"I'm right here!" Hisen called out behind him.

He had already finished his signs. Now he bent down and carefully placed a scroll on the water's surface.

"Summoning Jutsu! Ryurimaru, come forth!" he shouted.

A huge crimson and white koi fish leaped out of the lake. It was six times taller than a man, but there were even more wonders to come.

"Dragon god transform!" Hisen shouted again.

The koi instantly vanished behind a cloud of white smoke. Seconds later, a gigantic golden dragon appeared, with Hisen riding triumphantly on its back. The beast's long, snakelike body quickly wrapped around the masked man—and squeezed tight.

"No! How can you have such power?" he groaned, as his bones started to shatter.

Hisen jumped off the dragon's back and kneeled on the water. Though he was still pale and out of breath, he looked at the enemy and grinned.

"I'm almost done for, but so are you. Hell is opening its mouth for us—shall we go there together?"

"Y-you!" the man shouted. Just then a big blob of blood gurgled up from his throat, making his red mask look even redder. He quickly sank into the lake, leaving nothing behind but bubbles.

Hisen treaded water for a moment, making sure his enemy was truly dead. Then he turned to his son, who had been hiding under the massive Holy Tree in the center of the village.

"He's finished, Shibuki. Now I am too," Hisen said weakly, slowly sinking under. He bobbed up again a minute later, but he wasn't moving.

"Father!" Shibuki cried out, but he didn't rush to his aid. He just kept trembling inside his leafy haven.

That morning, Hisen had given his son strict orders before heading off to what would be his final battle.

"You need to watch this fight," he said. But Shibuki had completely ignored him, choosing safety over obedience.

Suddenly an old man with long white hair appeared on the shore. It was Senji, Hisen's aide and the village's former head ninja.

"No! Lord Hisen!!" he cried in horror, jumping into the lake. He swam rapidly toward Hisen, who was floating face down.

Too late. Senji sadly towed the dead body back to shore, then collapsed and started weeping.

"Lord Hisen! How could you die before this old man?" he sobbed, tears streaming down his craggy face.

All of a sudden he sensed someone watching him. Shibuki had finally crept out from his sanctuary and now stood shivering before the old man.

"D-don't cry, Senji," Shibuki begged. "If you cry, I won't know what to do..." The old man gave him a stern look.

"What are you saying, Lord Shibuki? Your father is dead. Now you must lead the village and protect the Hero's Water!"

"Who decided that?" Shibuki snapped.

"It's not a question of deciding. You are Lord Hisen's son. From now on, you are Lord Shibuki—"

"But I don't care about that stuff!" Shibuki spat out.

Senji started to reply, then saw Shibuki's angry face and quickly fell silent.

"Why me?" the young man wailed. "You know all about the village, Senji! You should be the leader!"

Before he could stop himself, the old man reached out and slapped his face. Stunned Shibuki put his hand on his cheek, which had turned dark red like an adzuki bean. The two gaped at each other for a moment. Then Shibuki ran away, pushing through the crowd of villagers who were streaming out of the Holy Tree.

"Senji is ashamed of you," the old man muttered. He looked sadly at the hand that had struck the boy, then fell next to Hisen's corpse and sobbed his heart out.

The Hidden Waterfall Village was in a precarious position. Unlike other hidden villages, they had never been led by a ninja of the elite kage rank. They didn't have a ninja army, either. But they did have something no other village possessed.

The Hidden Waterfall Village had a secret. This secret had helped them survive the Great Ninja War, a battle involving every hidden village in the world. But the secret that had once saved them soon became a magnet for big trouble, like the ninja who had just attacked Hisen.

Everybody wanted the secret and were willing to fight

for it. Ninja in the Hidden Waterfall had always been in short supply; now their ranks dwindled with each new battle. The few survivors that remained had been wounded beyond recovery. Now there were only two ninja left in the village: Senji, who had already retired, and Shibuki, who didn't really want to be one.

Six months after his father died, Shibuki visited the Hidden Leaf Village. The visit itself wasn't a big deal, just a courtesy call between allies. But when Shibuki asked for a special favor, his story took a different turn.

JUST A SIMPLE, C-RANK ASSIGNMENT

"Man, this job is boring," Naruto grumbled as he trudged down a steep mountain trail. His spiky yellow hair was even spikier than usual, which suited his foul mood.

"Quit complaining, Naruto! A C-rank assignment is important too!" Sakura snapped, glaring at him. She turned to smile adoringly at the dark-headed boy behind her.

"Right, Sasuke?" Sakura cooed, flipping back a lock of her pale pink hair. He quickly looked in the other direction.

"Sasuke! Sakura's talking to you!" Naruto whined. "Can't you at least answer her? Sheesh, you're always—"

Suddenly Naruto saw that Sakura had *that* look in her eyes, that I-love-Sasuke-and-I-don't-care-who-knows-it look.

"Sasuke is sooo irresistible," she sighed dreamily.

Naruto grunted and kicked a stone. It was business as usual for Squad Seven, a trio of ninja-in-training from the Hidden Leaf Village.

They were on their way to the Hidden Waterfall, a remote area they'd never seen before. Leading the group was Kakashi, their fearless sensei since they had graduated from the ninja academy. He was a genius ninja of jonin rank, just a step below kage. He always wore a black mask over most of his face.

Shibuki, the young man who had hired them, walked next to the sensei. He was as tall as Kakashi and had dark hair like Sasuke, but there the similarities ended. Though he was the leader of the Hidden Waterfall Village, Shibuki was not a powerful ninja. Truth be told, he was actually a bit of a wuss.

Shibuki was returning home after a visit to the Hidden Leaf Village. Too nervous to travel alone, he had asked for some ninja to guard him.

"Mind you, I don't expect any trouble," Shibuki had assured them. "But better to be safe than sorry."

Village ninja assignments were always ranked from A (the toughest) to D (the easiest). A C-rank assignment, like this one, was just a step above rescuing a cat from a gingko tree. The Hokage of the Hidden Leaf decided genin ninja—the lowest level—would do just fine for the mission. Since Squad Seven was free, they got the job.

The narrow path they had been descending suddenly opened out into a valley flanked by steep hills, with a swift stream flowing through the middle.

Shibuki glanced back at Naruto and the others.

"We'll be there soon," he said quietly.

"Good," Kakashi said, sounding relieved. "To tell the truth, we were getting a little worried."

"Worried?" Shibuki asked with surprise.

"Something like this happened before," Kakashi explained. "Once a client didn't let on that ninja were after him. We stuck by him anyway."

"You d-did?" Shibuki said shakily.

Kakashi stopped in his tracks and looked directly at Shibuki with his right eye. (His sharingan eye, as usual, was covered by his headband.)

"Of course. We ninja fulfill any assignments given to us," he said bluntly. "But we expect clients to tell us the truth. If someone's after you, we need to know."

Naruto suddenly rushed up, his face glowing with expectation. He'd been eavesdropping on their conversation and definitely liked what he'd heard.

"Sensei! Do you think something bad will happen

again?" he asked excitedly. "If another devil like Zabuza attacks us, this time I'll get him for sure."

Naruto was referring to Zabuza Momochi, a murderous rogue ninja they had fought on their very first assignment.

"Don't be an idiot, Naruto!" Kakashi snapped. "Things like that don't happen every day. Right, Mr. Shibuki?"

Shibuki swallowed hard. Kakashi started walking again, but Shibuki froze to the spot, paralyzed.

"What's with you?" Sasuke muttered, eyeing him suspiciously.

"Uh, n-nothing, nothing!" Shibuki sputtered, hurrying to catch up to Kakashi.

They started climbing a small hill. About halfway up,

they suddenly heard the sounds of rushing water. Intrigued, Naruto hurried to the top—then gaped in amazement.

"Whoa! Look at that!" he gasped, pointing at the breathtaking scene before him.

A spectacular waterfall splashed down a high cliff into a shimmering pond below. This pond fed the stream they had followed on their trek through the valley.

"Amazing! I've never seen anything like this, have you?" Sakura exclaimed, smiling back at Sasuke.

Sasuke was also transfixed by the incredible sight—until he noticed Sakura gawking at him with her jade green eyes.

"*Pfft*! No big deal," he scoffed, quickly turning away.

"You are sooo cute, Sasuke!" Sakura giggled. Sasuke frowned, and to his extreme embarrassment, started to blush.

"What's the matter, Sasuke? Your face is all red!" Naruto taunted.

"Sh-shut up," Sasuke snapped, but his cheeks still blazed like a Japanese maple in autumn.

"Mind your own business, Naruto!" Sakura hissed, jumping protectively in front of Sasuke. Naruto had been having a great time watching Sasuke squirm. Now he looked utterly dejected, like he'd just been told he was allergic to ramen, his favorite food.

Kakashi chuckled at the eternal triangle that was Squad Seven, but he sensed Shibuki was *not* amused.

"Just kid stuff," Kakashi assured him. "Please excuse their behavior."

"Are they really proper ninja?" Shibuki asked doubtfully.

"Well, I think they are each excellent in their own way," Kakashi said proudly.

"They are?" Shibuki gasped, looking back at Squad Seven again.

Sakura was chasing Naruto with her fists poised for pummeling, Naruto was whining and running away from her, while too-cool Sasuke was pretending not to notice. Kakashi chuckled again and turned to Shibuki.

"Believe it or not, those three have been through hell and back. Trust me, they are much more useful than they look."

But Shibuki still wasn't convinced. He just shook his head and started walking again.

"Hey, you two! That's enough!" Kakashi yelled at Naruto and Sakura. They reluctantly quit their cat-and-mouse game and fell in behind their sensei.

Now Shibuki took the lead, quickly striding along the

rocky ledges at the bottom of the waterfall. The area looked deserted, until they heard a small voice cry out.

"Lord Shibuki!"

Two little kids emerged from the woods near the cliff, smiling and waving at Shibuki. His usually grim expression softened as soon as he saw them.

"Shizuku! Himatsu!" he beamed, waving back. The kids nimbly scampered across the ledge. When they finally reached Shibuki, each one grabbed a leg and held on tight.

"Who are these guys, Lord Shibuki?" the boy Himatsu asked eagerly. He had a mop of black hair that was as spiky as Naruto's.

"Just guard ninja," Shibuki said dismissively. "I hired them at the Hidden Leaf." To hear Shibuki talk, Kakashi and Squad Seven were something akin to servants. Naruto gave him a hard stare.

"What's with you?" he groused. "You were shakin' in your boots a little while ago."

"Take it easy, Naruto!" Kakashi urged. "He's not lying, after all. We *are* here to guard him."

Naruto frowned at his sensei.

"I know. I just don't like him," he muttered.

"Let it go, kid. We can't choose clients on whether we

like them or not," Kakashi reminded him. He glanced back at Shibuki, who was beaming down at the children still clinging to him.

"What are you two doing here?" Shibuki asked, patting their heads. The little girl Shizuku proudly spoke up.

"It's my turn to clean the pond today! My brother is helping me!"

"Why, thank you, Shizuku," Shibuki said kindly, giving her brown pigtails a gentle tug. He gazed out at the water.

All kinds of flotsam floated on the surface: crumpled snack bags, empty cans, chopsticks that had seen better days. Shibuki surveyed the damage for a while, then turned to Kakashi with a question in his eyes.

"What's up?" Kakashi asked in his usual lazy drawl.

"Could they help clean the pond?" Shibuki asked, pointing to Squad Seven. Needless to say, the idea didn't exactly thrill them.

"What? You want us to pick up trash?" Naruto griped. He looked offended at the very suggestion.

"In the water? But I'll get all wet," Sakura whined.

Sasuke kept quiet as usual, but his glaring eyes spoke volumes. Kakashi sighed and slumped his shoulders.

"I suppose they *could* help," he said tiredly. "But you only hired us to guard you to the Hidden Waterfall Village.

Anything extra you'll pay for, okay?"

"No problem," Shibuki said. Kakashi nodded and turned to his students.

"Get to work, crew. Please."

"Whaaaat?" the three whined in unison. How could their sensei sell them out like that? But rules were rules, and they knew griping would get them absolutely nowhere. Just like Kakashi said, ninja always fulfill their assignments, be it battling bad guys or scooping up dog poo.

Cursing Shibuki under their breaths, they waded into the water to begin their odious task. Kakashi sat nearby, where he could keep an eye on them, then pulled a small red book out of his pack. *Make-out Violence* was the latest installment of Kakashi's all-time favorite series. On the cover, a pretty girl punched out a guy who was holding a big bouquet of daisies. (Evidently she preferred tulips.) Not exactly *The Tale of Genji*, but Kakashi liked it.

Shibuki stood nearby, quietly watching the clean-up.

"So what's the deal?" Kakashi said casually, flipping through the pages to find his place.

"Huh?" Shibuki stuttered. He glanced nervously at Kakashi, who had already started reading.

"You don't really need their help, do you?" Kakashi said as he turned a page.

"Uh, I..." Shibuki hesitated. Kakashi pressed on for an answer.

"I can see how tense you are," he observed. "You obviously want us to stay. What do you have in mind?"

"N-nothing," Shibuki stammered. "You can go home right after the clean-up. I'll send your money along later."

Kakashi closed *Make-out Violence* and cleared his throat before he replied.

"I've heard rumors that shinobi from other lands are active near this village."

Shibuki's right eyebrow twitched a tiny bit.

"Tsk! Rumors like that have been around a long time," he scoffed.

"I've also heard that your father lost his life fighting intruders," Kakashi said quietly.

Just then a shadow crossed their faces. They looked up to see a large brown bird circling above them.

"Hmmm. That bird's from the Hidden Leaf," Kakashi noted. The blood instantly drained from Shibuki's face.

"Wh-why is it here?" he croaked.

"Nothing to worry about," Kakashi assured him. "Just a messenger bird. Must be something urgent."

He stood up and put out his arm. The bird swooped down and landed, a tiny scroll tied to its leg. Kakashi quickly scanned the message with a troubled expression, scratching his silvery head.

"I'm being summoned to an emergency meeting," he finally announced. "Sorry, Mr. Shibuki, I'll have to leave right away."

"Already?" Shibuki shuddered.

"Yup. But our assignment here is over anyway," Kakashi shrugged. He called out to Squad Seven, who were still toiling away in the pond.

"I have to return to the village, guys. Come back when you're done, okay?"

"Yessss, sir!" Naruto shouted, punching his fist in the air.

27

"What? You're leaving now?" Sakura said, raising her eyebrows. Sasuke just nodded. He was never one to waste words when a grunt or a glare would do.

Kakashi brushed off his beige vest, waved good-bye, and instantly vanished from the scene. Shibuki gaped after him in shock.

How can he move so fast? he wondered.

A GATHERING OF ENEMIES

In the dark woods above the waterfall, a gang of ninja kneeled before a rock. They wore identical gray uniforms with shuriken symbols on the back, but no headbands to indicate their allegiance. Nearby, three ninja dressed in different garb nervously paced around. No one said a word while they waited for their leader to appear.

"Well! Looks like everybody's here," a gruff voice finally said. A man in a long gray coat swaggered onto the scene, scratching his dark goatee. His black hair stuck out around his head like peacock feathers.

"Suien-san," the group murmured, lowering their heads with respect. Suien sat down on the rock and looked them over with a critical eye.

"Do you understand the plan?" he asked in a low tone.

A lovely young woman nodded her head.

"Yes," she said quietly.

Hisame was a kunoichi, a female ninja, the only one in the group. While the other ninja looked drab, she sported a strapless corset, skintight pants, and a flowing jacket that bared her shoulders. Usually ninja try to blend in with their surroundings, but Hisame's stylish outfit screamed, "Look at me, everybody! Look at me!"

"We already blocked the road here," she confidently told Suien. "That Kakashi and his sharingan will have a hard time getting back here."

"Nice work, Hisame," Suien said, beaming at her. She bowed deeply to him.

"I never imagined the famous Kakashi would set foot in this little village," Suien said with wonder.

"I'd really love to fight him sometime," Hisame admitted. "But having Kakashi here now would only make this harder. Lucky for us, he went back to the Hidden Leaf."

A tall, nasty-looking man kneeled beside her. He had a thick line of green paint across his nose, which made him look even nastier.

"You were right, Suien-san," Murasame said. "There are no guards at the village entrance. Just say the word, and we'll invade with our underlings."

"Not so fast, Murasame," Suien scolded. "We should

enter the village secretly at first."

"But, but..." Murasame protested.

Just then a slimy-looking guy in gray overalls slithered forward and leered at his comrade.

"You're so hot-blooded, Murasame! Not good, not good," he purred. Kirisame was Suien's third henchman. Like Kakashi, he wore a black mask over most of his face.

"You should talk, Kirisame," Murasame snapped. "You love blood more than any of us!"

"I do like to fight," Kirisame admitted, twirling his kunai. "But you charge in without thinking, Murasame. I wait patiently before I go in for the kill."

As if to prove his bloodlust, Kirisame abruptly sliced his thumb open. A thin line of bright red blood seeped out. Kirisame hungrily licked it off, like it was some delicious tonkatsu sauce.

"Remember, Kirisame, we want to capture the villagers, not kill them," Suien warned. "Hurt them if you must, but no murder unless it's strictly necessary."

Kirisame clearly didn't agree, and slinked toward Suien with his fists clenched.

"But I *came* here for the killing!" he whined. "I can't believe you, Suien-san! I know this is your hometown, but c'mon! You've raised hell at other villages."

Hisame glared at him. She looked even more beautiful when she was peeved. "Don't be stupid!" she hissed. "Who knows where the water is hidden? We can't search every house. We can only take hostages and make them talk."

Suien nodded at her with approval. "You're right on target, Hisame. Now I understand why they called you the sharpest ninja of the Hidden Rain Village."

Hisame smiled up at him.

"Please don't call me that," she said coyly. "I dumped my Hidden Rain name a long time ago." Suien smirked at her before getting back to business.

"Only the village leaders know where the Hero's Water is hidden," he continued. "We do *not* want to make them mad." Suien narrowed his beady eyes at Kirisame, who quickly backed away.

"Sorry, Suien-san," he muttered.

"Try to understand, Kirisame," Suien explained. "Once we get the goods, you can do whatever your little heart desires."

Kirisame's face lit up with joy. He dearly loved wreaking havoc the way some people dearly love growing bonsai.

"Heh! That's good to know!" he chortled, stabbing the air for practice.

"Sheesh! And you were complaining about me! You're hopeless," Murasame sighed.

"Oh, yeah?" Kirisame snapped, marching toward him. Then he saw Suien's angry face and skidded to a stop.

"Now keep still for the next few hours," Suien warned them. He faced each of his gang in turn, then punched his right fist in the air.

"Okay, comrades! Go do what you need to do!" he commanded.

While the ninja took off for parts unknown, Suien rubbed his hands together and smiled.

"Well, Shibuki! You used to be my student. Let's see how you've grown since then..."

Then Suien vanished too.

ROCK AND ROLL!

"Are we finally finished? I'm starvin'!" Naruto griped, wiping his forehead. They had filled countless bags with trash, and now the pond actually looked quite clean.

"Agh, I'm tired! I can't believe Sensei took this job without asking us first," Sakura moaned. She was stretched out on a rock at the edge of the water.

"Is that it?" Sasuke asked Shibuki. The young leader was helping the children, but he stopped to examine the pond.

"Yeah, looks good. You can leave now," he said curtly.

"'You can leave now'? That's it?" Naruto sputtered, rolling up his sleeves. If anyone deserved a punch in the snoot, Shibuki surely did.

"I'm paying you, remember? That should be enough," Shibuki pointed out, but that wasn't enough for Naruto.

"Who cares about money? Don't you have anything else to say?" he persisted.

Sakura pushed Naruto aside. Inside, she was hopping mad, but she gave Shibuki her best fake smile.

"Naruto's right, Mr. Shibuki. Can we rest here before we leave?" she suggested mildly.

"Sorry. You need to go now," Shibuki said firmly. Naruto got right in his face.

"I can't believe how you talk to us!" he said hotly. "So what if you're the leader of the Hidden Waterfall? You don't have to act so stuck-up!"

"Cut it out, you two," Sasuke muttered from the background. Naruto and Sakura swung around with surprise, but Sasuke wasn't kidding around.

"C'mon. Let's take off," he ordered.

"Oh, yeah? Why should we?" Naruto challenged, jutting out his elbows.

"Um, he's right, Sasuke. Maybe we should stick around for a while," Sakura said uncertainly. She hated to disagree with the world's cutest ninja-in-training.

Sasuke ignored them both and headed for the path leading back to the Hidden Leaf Village.

"Sasuke! Wait up!" Sakura yelled, waving her arms wildly.

Just then a loud voice boomed out from nearby.

"You're back, Lord Shibuki? Why didn't you tell me?"

Everybody turned to look, even Sasuke. An old man with long white hair shuffled toward Shibuki, gasping for breath with his every faltering step.

Shibuki immediately bolted away, but he didn't get far. Soon the old man, whose name was Senji, was clinging to Shibuki's back.

"You can't leave now, Lord Shibuki!" he cried desperately. "As the village leader of Hidden Waterfall, you must—"

"Shut up, Senji!" Shibuki snapped, wriggling away from him. Before the old man could protest any further, Shibuki quickly made his escape.

"Hey, you! Wait a minute!" Naruto yelled after him. Shibuki turned and glared, but Naruto wasn't backing off.

"You can't leave now! What if Grandpa gets hurt?"

"Don't worry about us! This is our problem!" Senji insisted.

"But, but..." Naruto sputtered helplessly. For once, words failed him as he gaped at the old man.

Shibuki watched them for a moment, then started to walk away again. Senji tottered after him.

"What's with them?" Naruto huffed.

"Mind your own business, Naruto," Sasuke said coldly. "The geezer's right. This has nothing to do with us."

"But just look at him! We have to do something!" Naruto protested, pointing to Senji, who had just stumbled over a rock. When Sasuke didn't reply, Naruto turned to Sakura for support.

"C'mon, Sakura! You know I'm right," he urged.

"Uh, I guess so," Sakura said vaguely, inspecting her fingernails.

She glanced at Sasuke, trying to figure out what he was thinking. Sasuke turned and headed down the path, and after a second's hesitation, Sakura followed.

"Sakuraaaaa! Sheesh!" Naruto groused. Sakura looked back at him and shrugged.

Naruto sighed dramatically, then joined them. But as they trekked away from the Hidden Waterfall, he refused to let the matter rest.

"Why did Shibuki wanna get rid of us so fast? And why are you playing it so cool, Sasuke? Aren't you curious?"

Sasuke, who was in the lead, calmly answered.

"It's simple. Shibuki didn't want to show us the way to his village."

"Huh?"

"You're right, Sasuke! We never even saw where he lives," Sakura said thoughtfully.

"All that trash was in the water for a reason. The village must lie above the waterfall. There's definitely a path up to that cliff."

Naruto turned and looked behind him. To his surprise, the waterfall had disappeared from view. They didn't call it the Hidden Waterfall Village for nothing.

"*Pfft*! I figured that out a long time ago," he fibbed. "But Shibuki still didn't have to act so snippy."

"Like I said, not our problem," Sasuke shrugged, picking up the pace, but Naruto still looked troubled.

"I dunno. There's just something weird about the guy."

They hiked in silence for a while on the path that followed the stream. Soon the path veered away from the water, and they started the uphill surge to the mountain. They hadn't climbed far when Sasuke, who'd been tearing along at his usual brisk clip, suddenly put on the brakes.

"Hold it, everybody," he said firmly.

"What's wrong?" Sakura asked with surprise. Did Sasuke finally change his mind about helping the old man? She hoped so, but Sasuke only pointed at the hill above them.

"Check out all those little rocks," he said.

Sakura and Naruto looked up. Small brown pebbles were rolling down like marbles. Not exactly a fascinating

sight, but Sakura quickly got the implication.

"Oh, no! Does that mean—" she gasped, covering her mouth with both hands.

"Will somebody pleeeease tell me what's goin' on?" Naruto begged. Sakura glared back at him.

"Don't you see, idiot? The hill is about to—"

Suddenly they heard a loud rumble, the sound of trees being ripped from their roots.

"This is bad! Run!" Sasuke yelled. He sped back in the direction of the waterfall, followed by Sakura.

But Naruto stood frozen to the spot, gaping up in horror. A huge boulder tumbled down the hill, mowing down everything in its path.

"W-waaaaah!" Naruto shrieked, darting away.

The boulder reached the path and immediately went after Squad Seven. Lucky for them, it wasn't rolling too fast. Then, just when they thought they were safe, another boulder barreled toward them from the opposite direction. There was only one place to retreat.

"Aggh!" Sasuke groaned, as he vaulted onto the slower rock. Naruto quickly leaped up on the other one. But poor Sakura flinched for a microsecond and lost her chance to escape.

"Hellllp!" she screamed, looking wildly from boulder

to boulder. Naruto and Sasuke instantly jumped down and stood protectively on either side of her.

"Can you do it, Naruto?" Sasuke yelled.

"Yep! How 'bout you?" Naruto shouted. He quickly started to make signs, then shouted again.

"Multi-Shadow Clone!"

Dozens of Naruto clones showed up with their arms extended in front of them. As they struggled to hold back the boulders, Sasuke jumped out with Sakura in his arms. He gently set her down, then threw a kunai with a paper bomb tied to it into the ground beside the biggest rock.

The bomb exploded with a bang, sending the two rocks tumbling toward the stream. They hit the water with a big splash and finally rolled to a stop.

"Whew!" the clones gasped, wiping their foreheads before they vanished in a cloud of smoke. Only the real Naruto was left, exhausted and dripping with sweat. He glanced over at the stream and saw Sasuke crawling onto a boulder.

"Sasuke! What's wrong?" Naruto yelled.

Sasuke didn't answer. He carefully inspected the rock, then bent down to smell its surface.

"Anything suspicious?" Sakura asked seriously, jumping up beside him.

"Take a whiff," Sasuke directed, as he kept on sniffing. "Explosives smell like this. Big explosives. The kind used for large-scale blasting."

Sakura put her nose to the rock and inhaled.

"You're right," she said, frowning.

"So what the heck does that mean?" Naruto demanded to know. He was standing on the shore, feeling very left out.

"Someone caused this landslide on purpose!" Sakura shouted down at him.

"Huh?"

Sasuke hopped down and landed beside Naruto. He stared pensively at the ground before he finally spoke.

"This definitely was not an act of nature," he said quietly. "Somebody blew up that mountain."

"Why? Why would they do that?" Naruto asked desperately.

"Beats me," Sasuke shrugged. "But one thing is crystal clear: something really bad is about to happen."

Sakura came down from the rock with a worried look on her face. She excelled at quickly grasping situations, and what she grasped now really bothered her.

"Now the only road to the village is blocked," she pointed out. "Which could mean one of two things: they don't want to let people out, or they don't want to let people in."

Sasuke looked back in the direction of the village and reflected for a moment.

"Maybe both," he concluded at last. "In any case, the guys who did this will take their next step real soon."

Naruto had been trying hard to follow along, but a big question mark was lodged firmly in his brain.

"I still don't get this! Will somebody pleeease explain?" he burst out.

"Actually, it's pretty simple, Naruto. The Hidden Waterfall Village is in danger," Sakura sighed. Naruto reacted to the news with his usual get-up-and-go.

"Then why are we still standin' here? We gotta go help 'em!" he shrieked, running back toward the waterfall. But Sasuke wasn't ready to sound the battle cry.

"Sasuke! Aren't you coming too?" Naruto shouted back at him.

"Nope," Sasuke said firmly. "Like I said before, we have no obligation to help them."

Naruto gaped at him in disbelief.

"How can you say that? That wimp Shibuki doesn't even know about this yet! We gotta go tell him right—"

"Don't you remember? He told us to leave them alone,"

Sasuke said.

"So what? *I'm* gonna help the Hidden Waterfall!" Naruto vowed, blasting off like a bottle rocket.

THE HERO AND THE WUSS

Naruto kept on running until he reached the waterfall. Then he slowly turned around, hoping to see the rest of his squad, but...

"No way! Not even Sakura?" Naruto fumed, stamping his foot. He would have loved to throw a full-blown tantrum, but unfortunately, there wasn't time. Naruto needed to find the way into the village.

"Must be somewhere around here," he muttered, scanning the general area. He saw rocky ledges and plenty of greenery, but nothing that looked like an entrance.

Stumped, Naruto sat down on a big flat rock near the pond. Suddenly he heard a faraway voice over the sound of cascading water.

"Shibuki! Shibuki!"

So the poor old guy is still looking for him, Naruto thought. *Shibuki is such a jerk.*

Just then Naruto felt a presence nearby. He jumped up

and ducked behind another rock. Then he peeked out and saw Shibuki, who was climbing one of the rock walls that flanked the waterfall.

"Yo, Shibuki!" Naruto yelled.

Shibuki shrieked and kept on shrieking as he slid down the wall on his bare hands. Needless to say, he was not delighted to see the kid in the orange jumpsuit.

"You again? Thought you left already!" Shibuki snapped.

"We can't go home now, even if we wanted to," Naruto said. He quickly told Shibuki about the landslide, sparing none of the dramatic details.

Shibuki looked stricken at the news and started trembling from head to toe. Even his teeth were chattering.

"Whoa! Are you scared or somethin'?" Naruto asked innocently.

"N-no way! Why sh-should I be?" Shibuki stammered.

"But you're shakin' all over!" Naruto pointed out.

"S-sure I am! I'm sh-shaking with anticipation!" Shibuki insisted. He stood up straight as a chopstick, but his brave warrior act was clearly a sham.

"Hey, here's an idea!" Naruto said brightly, snapping his fingers. "Since you're the village leader, you should go tell everybody!"

"T-tell them what?"

"What I just told you, silly! Some guys blew up the mountain path. Things are kinda dangerous right now."

Shibuki glared at him.

"I don't need you to tell me what to do," he said in a haughty tone. He turned away from Naruto and started to scale the wall again.

"Where are you going now?" Naruto called after him.

"None of your business," Shibuki grumbled. "Just leave me alone, Naru—"

Just then they heard an agonized cry from above.

"Lord Shibuki!"

Naruto and Shibuki jerked up their heads. A small man teetered at the very edge of the cliff, wildly waving his arms at them. Before he could say anything else, he fell.

The man plummeted down for three horrifying seconds, then hit the ground with a heavy thud. Shibuki frantically dashed over to him.

"Wh-what happened?" he gasped, helping him to his feet. The man spoke haltingly, struggling for breath.

"The...enemies..."

"How did they find the entrance?" Shibuki gently persisted.

"I...don't...know. But...the...village...is..."

The man tried to go on, but his life force was fading fast. He was too weak to even hold up his head.

"H-hey, pull yourself together! Tell me what happened!" Shibuki urged, shaking his shoulders.

There was no answer. The man gasped one last time and slumped against Shibuki. It was over.

Shibuki shivered as he slowly lowered the corpse to the ground. Then he looked at his hand and screamed.

"B-blood..." Shibuki shuddered.

"We have to hurry," Naruto said seriously. Shibuki gave him a dazed look.

"That man risked his life to warn you," Naruto quickly went on. "If we don't get to the village soon, he'll die in vain."

Naruto grabbed Shibuki's shoulders, trying to make him stand, but the young leader just crumpled to the ground.

"I c-can't take this anymore," he sobbed, staring at the dead body. Just then the old man named Senji straggled out of the woods.

"Oh, there you are, Lord Shibuki," he said with relief. "I've been looking all over for—"

Just then Senji saw the body. He froze for a split second, then hobbled toward the corpse.

"Who...who is he?" Senji stuttered, looking into the man's face. He cried out when he finally recognized him.

"Not you, Noji! How could this happen?"

"The village may be under attack," Naruto told him.

Senji looked up in surprise.

"What?"

"We think someone cooked up a landslide to block the road here," Naruto quickly explained. "The villagers need your help!"

Senji nodded vigorously.

"Indeed. Thank you for warning me," he said sincerely.

Naruto happily jerked his thumb at his chest, which was puffed out to the max with pride.

"I'll come along too!" he said with enthusiasm.

Senji didn't exactly jump at Naruto's generous offer. He looked down and shuffled his feet in the dirt.

"Uh, I appreciate that, but..." the old man stalled.

"Why can't I help?" Naruto asked plaintively. Senji ignored Naruto's pleading face and tried to explain.

"The Hidden Waterfall Village has stayed peaceful because this cliff protects us," he said gravely. "But we have another secret as well—a very dangerous secret."

Naruto's ears perked up. This lowly C-rank assign-

ment was getting cooler by the minute. Senji took a deep breath and continued.

"Even though the Hidden Leaf is our ally, we still can't let you near the hiding place. Please leave now."

Naruto just stood for a minute with his mouth open, letting it all sink in. Then he blew up.

"But I've already been this far! I can't pretend I didn't see anything!" Naruto snapped. He marched right over to the rock wall and started to climb.

"W-wait, please!" Senji pleaded.

"Leave me alone! I'll go on my own!"

"No!" Senji protested.

But Naruto was determined, and not even a steaming bowl of ramen could change his mind. (Not that there were any noodles in the vicinity, but still...)

Naruto was about halfway to the top when he heard Shibuki's shrill voice. He couldn't quite make out what Shibuki was saying, but the guy definitely sounded confused.

What a wimp, Naruto thought.

Soon he reached the top, right near the spot where the villager fell. Naruto quickly spotted a small opening to what appeared to be a cave.

"Bingo!" he crowed, hustling inside.

In contrast to its tiny entrance, the cave was actually

quite large, with several small ponds glowing with green-ish water.

"Is this it?" Naruto muttered to himself.

"Yes," Senji sighed from behind Naruto.

Naruto swung around with shock.

"How did you—?"

Senji shrugged and continued.

"Tell no one what you see here," he said gravely.

"Right!" Naruto promised, giving Senji the thumbs-up sign. Suddenly Shibuki strode past them, looking deadly serious.

"This way. Hurry," he said tersely, before jumping into the nearest pond.

The water looked too shallow to hide anyone, but Shibuki quickly disappeared from sight. Naruto was squinting at the pond, trying to see underwater, when he felt two strong hands placed firmly on his back.

"Please hurry," Senji urged, giving Naruto a big push. Naruto only had time for a single word before he fell in.

"Huh?????"

As he plunged through the water, Naruto realized the pond was much deeper than had it seemed; in fact, he couldn't even see the bottom.

Senji, who had dived in after Naruto, now passed

him in the water. Naruto followed him through the murky depths until a tunnel appeared on one side, illuminated by an eerie light. Shibuki entered the tunnel first, followed by Senji and Naruto.

They swam a short distance, until the tunnel emptied into a large lagoon filled with gigantic tree roots and rotting leaves. Naruto had been swimming underwater for a while, and his lungs were crying for mercy. He zoomed to the surface, stuck his head out—and gaped in utter astonishment.

"What...what is this place?" Naruto whispered, looking around with wonder. The view was indeed magnificent.

They were now in a lake at the top of the cliff. On a small island in the center stood the biggest tree Naruto had ever seen. Its stately branches formed a giant umbrella that blocked out half the sky.

Naruto just gazed contentedly for a moment, until something on the lakefront caught his eye. Was that smoke over there? He blinked and looked again.

"What the—?"

Every house in the Hidden Waterfall Village was on fire, while a gang of ninja chased the screaming villagers. Some poor villagers were already on the ground, their hands tied firmly behind them.

"No, Lord Shibuki! Don't go!" Senji yelled. Naruto turned to see Senji diving back into the water. Shibuki was nowhere to be seen.

"Aw, forget about him!" Naruto grumbled, focusing all of his chakra on his feet. He gave the water one swift kick and took off flying. Naruto reached the shore in one big leap, landing right in the middle of the attackers.

They quickly surrounded him, but Naruto kept his cool, rapidly making a sign. In an instant, dozens of Naruto clones showed up, ready for action. The ninja gaped at the brigade of orange jumpsuits.

"Ready or not, here we come!" the Narutos yelled and, without further ado, beat the heck out of the enemy.

BAD THINGS COME IN THREES

The Naruto clones stood with their hands on their hips, grinning at the messy heaps of knocked-down ninja. Then they vanished as quickly as they had arrived, leaving only the real Naruto behind. He beamed at the frightened villagers.

"Relax! You're all okay now!" he said reassuringly, but the villagers still looked bewildered.

"W-where's Lord Shibuki?" a small voice piped up from the middle of the crowd.

"Huh?"

"Lord Shibuki! Where is he fighting?"

"That scaredy-cat? Who knows?" Naruto snorted. "We were together earlier, but then he—"

Just then Naruto felt something hard hit the side of his head. He swung around wildly and saw the little boy

Himatsu glaring at him. Clutched in his small hand was another stone.

"Lord Shibuki is Lord Hisen's son! A hero's son is a hero!" Himatsu yelled, tears streaming down his cheeks.

"Hey! D-don't throw that, okay?" Naruto stuttered.

Himatsu raised his arm and kept on glaring at him. Just then a plump woman emerged from the crowd and grabbed the little boy's arms.

"No, Himatsu! Stop this!" she said harshly.

"But Lord Shibuki is a hero, Mama!" Himatsu cried.

"Ninja go home!" shouted someone else.

Another stone hit Naruto's back, then another got him in the leg. Naruto couldn't tell who the culprits were, but

nobody tried to stop them.

"Wh-why are you doin' this?" Naruto cried out.

Just then somebody screamed bloody murder. The terrified villagers ran off in every direction.

"Calm down!" Naruto warned, quickly preparing himself for battle. The atmosphere quickly turned dark and very evil. Something wicked was definitely coming his way.

All of a sudden, a villager fell forward, a kunai stuck in his back. Naruto hurried to him and gently pulled out the blade. Surprisingly, the wound wasn't much more than a scratch. The man was unconscious, but his life wasn't in danger.

"Crap! It really stinks that we can't just kill 'em!" a voice growled from nearby. Naruto looked up.

Hoo-boy, he thought.

A tall man with a green stripe across his nose stalked through the fray of frenzied villagers. He noticed Naruto gaping at him and frowned.

"Who's this little brat?" he snapped.

"Remember, Murasame? He's with that Kakashi guy. Why do you care anyway?" another ninja replied, his mouth covered by a black mask.

Just then a beautiful kunoichi glided toward them, looking like she'd just arrived at a garden party.

"Don't dismiss the blond kid, Kirisame. He knows jutsu far beyond his years," she said smoothly.

"My name ain't 'the blond kid,' lady!" Naruto huffed, glaring at her. "It's Naruto Uzumaki! Remember that!"

Murasame sadly shook his head at the fallen ninja, then glanced at Naruto with new respect.

"Well, Hisame! If you say so, it must be true!" he told her. "We should probably kill him first."

"Ooooh, let's!" Kirisame said eagerly, skulking toward Naruto. Hisame quickly joined him, after making sure her blue earrings were securely fastened.

These guys are definitely capable, Naruto thought, but they didn't really scare him. Something told him he was just as good as they were, or maybe even better.

Suddenly Murasame darted past the others, aiming his kunai. Naruto leaped out of the way. The blade ripped through the spot where he'd been standing and lightly grazed his cheek.

"Yowwwww!" Naruto shrieked, grabbing his own weapon. He was not about to lose this fight.

He lunged at Murasame, who lost his balance. Naruto seized the opportunity to shove his knee in Murasame's stomach. Murasame swiftly crossed his arms, trying to blunt the attack, but Naruto's raw power sent him flying.

As Murasame somersaulted backward, he threw another kunai in Naruto's direction. Naruto easily evaded it and concentrated all of his chakra on his right hand.

"Woo hoo!" he yelled, charging at Murasame.

"Tsk! You don't impress me!" Murasame scoffed, as Naruto's kunai ripped through the front of his sleeveless shirt. Sadly, Murasame's ugly mug was still intact, including the stupid green stripe over his nose.

"This kid is unbelievable," he muttered.

"Oh, dear! Is Mr. Murasame losing to a little boy?" Kirisame mocked. Murasame glowered at him.

"Shut your trap!" he spat out. He quickly made another sign, concentrating chakra all over his body.

"Here I come! Can you see me?" Murasame shouted.

Naruto choked at the freakish sight coming his way. Trailing behind Murasame were dozens of afterimages, looking like some ghostly chorus line. Naruto whirled his head away, but the images stayed with him, blurring his vision. He had no idea where the real Murasame was, but he soon found out.

"*Ooof*!" Naruto grunted as a fist slammed into his gut. He sailed through the air and landed a short distance away. Naruto rubbed his eyes and looked again, but the weird apparitions still remained.

"Don't be fooled, Naruto! That's genjutsu!" a familiar voice shouted from above.

Naruto swung up his head. Sakura was perched atop a nearby building, nervously looking down at him.

"Ha! My jutsu is impossible to break!" Murasame sniggered, aiming his kunai. He roared with laughter as he ran toward Naruto, but what happened next wasn't so funny.

Murasame gasped as his afterimages suddenly dissolved. Then a strong force propelled him all the way to the lake, where he fell in with a noisy splash.

"Difficult, but not impossible," Sasuke said matter-of-factly. He glared at Hisame and Kirisame with his elbows out, ready for action.

"Sasuke!" Naruto cried with joy. Suddenly he remembered how Sasuke had ditched him back on the trail.

"So! You finally decided to show up, eh?" Naruto huffed.

"Tsk! I'm not some fool who charges in before I check out the enemy," Sasuke said with a shrug.

"So I'm a fool, huh?" Naruto hissed.

"Fool, idiot, dunce, pick one."

"Right here, right now!" Naruto barked, putting up his dukes.

"Stop bickering, you brats! We don't like being messed

with like this!" Hisame screeched. How dare they keep her waiting! Didn't they know who she was?

Meanwhile, Kirisame's eyes sparkled with anticipation as he licked the blade of his kunai.

"My, my! My work load seems to be increasing," he cackled, creeping forward like a spider crab. Naruto sensed his movements and moved into battle position.

"Let's get them first and settle this later," he grumbled, but Sasuke shook his head.

"You keep out of this," he said firmly.

"But why?" Naruto whined. Sasuke glanced back at him.

"Just rest," he urged. Then Sasuke swung around and glared at Kirisame and Hisame.

"I can handle these two myself," he muttered, loud enough for them to hear. Hisame was plainly outraged.

"How *dare* you say that, kid!" she sniveled.

"Thanks to this idiot, I know just how sharp you guys are," Sasuke replied. Then he grinned.

"Go ahead, attack me from anywhere," Sasuke challenged. They instantly accepted his invitation.

Hisame ran up and gently stroked Sasuke's arm, just like she was petting a cat. Hidden in her hand was a senbon, a long thin acupuncture needle. Sasuke easily knocked

it away with his kunai, then ducked as another kunai sailed toward him, courtesy of Kirisame.

Now Sasuke roughly grabbed Hisame's arm. She tried to push him away, but fell right on her sorry butt. Sasuke quickly stepped away, but Hisame was right on his tail.

"Enough of this childish stuff," she hissed, jumping to her feet. She lunged at Sasuke's back with another senbon, while Kirisame hurled another kunai at him.

Sasuke easily knocked them both down with a few swift moves. They hit the ground with matching thuds, glaring at Sasuke with pure hatred. Suddenly another kunai soared through the air and pierced the ground near Sasuke's feet.

"Well! Wasn't that a sight?" Murasame sneered from behind, but Sasuke was ready and waiting for him. Several seconds passed, but Murasame didn't budge.

"What's the holdup? Are you tired or something?" Sasuke scoffed.

"Yeah! Tired of *you*, scumbag!" Murasame cracked, pointing his kunai. He took a swipe at Sasuke's neck, just as Naruto charged him from the side. Though Sasuke's jutsu was more refined, Naruto handily beat him in the brute force department. He pushed Murasame to the ground and pounced on him. But what Naruto thought was Murasame was just a big gnarly tree branch.

"Blast!" Naruto sputtered, rolling away to dodge another flying dagger. The kunai stabbed the branch and split it right down the middle. Naruto scrambled to his feet and joined his comrade. Sasuke glanced at him nervously as they waited for the next attack.

"Uh, thanks," he finally mumbled in a low voice.

"Huh? Say what?" Naruto gasped, gaping at him.

"I *said* thank you," Sasuke snapped. Naruto chortled with glee.

"Whoa! That's so not like you!"

"Whatever," Sasuke muttered, turning back to the battle.

Hisame and Kirisame were again on their feet, but keeping their distance. Now Murasame joined them, looking more than a little peeved.

"Guess we underestimated them," he muttered.

"Ya think?" Hisame snapped. "That Kakashi is their sensei. No wonder they fight so well."

But Kirisame just chuckled behind his mask.

"That Kakashi ain't comin' back, remember?"

Sakura, who had been watching from the roof, gasped as the puzzle pieces quickly snapped into place.

"Now I get it! That landslide was meant to keep Kakashi-sensei from coming back!"

Sasuke heard her and nodded gravely. But Naruto, as usual, was brimming with confidence.

"So what if Sensei's not here?" he said breezily. "We can beat these thugs easy!"

"Don't get carried away, Naruto. They still have some aces up their sleeves," Sasuke muttered. Naruto fixed his gaze on the enemy and frowned.

"I know," he finally admitted.

"C'mon! Let's get both of them!" Murasame barked. He started making signs, filling his body with chakra in a different way than before.

Suddenly he yelled, "Acceleration Method!" and dashed forward with incredible speed. One second later he was attacking Naruto and Sasuke with his kunai. They managed to dodge his blows, but it wasn't easy.

"Ahhhh! This feels so good!" Murasame sighed in ecstasy. Compressed chakra radiated from his whole body, making him even faster.

"We've gotta get this guy!" Naruto sputtered.

"Don't be too hasty," Sasuke cautioned. "If he keeps blowing through chakra like this, he'll run out real soon."

Just then Sasuke looked in the background. Kirisame and Hisame were making signs at a rapid pace, which meant that Act Two was about to commence.

"I get it! He was buying time so his comrades could use their jutsu!" Sasuke shouted to Naruto.

"Huh?" Naruto mumbled.

"Too late, little boy!" Murasame grinned, jumping out of the way as Hisame and Kirisame stepped forward. They had been stocking up on chakra and were now ready to rumble.

"Water Style: Rapid Thunder Whip Jutsu!" they shouted, dipping their first two fingers into the lake. A pair of long water ropes wriggled up from the surface. Hisame and Kirisame grabbed the ends and started swinging them around like whips.

"Die, ya little punks!" Hisame shrieked.

The water whips looked innocuous enough, but they were as sharp as samurai swords. Hisame and Kirisame gaily slashed down trees and grass as they headed for their prey.

With two quick, well-timed jumps, Naruto and Sasuke managed to avoid getting hit. They threw kunai at Hisame and Kirisame, who easily flicked them away. Still airborne, Naruto and Sasuke put their hands and feet together and pushed hard. Then Sasuke made a sign and took a deep breath.

"Fire Style: Fireball Jutsu!" he shouted.

Red flames came roaring out of Sasuke's mouth. He turned his head toward Kirisame and kept on making signs. Kirisame tried to shield himself with the water whip, but Sasuke's fireball instantly vaporized it.

"Who cares? Plenty more where that came from!" Kirisame snorted, plunging his fingers into the water again. Though Sasuke's plan had failed, Kirisame was still impressed.

"How can a kid know this jutsu?" he growled. Kirisame waited for the fireball to go out, then swung his whip at Sasuke again.

"No way!" Naruto shrieked, charging at him. Kirisame turned away from Sasuke and struck the ground once with his whip, transforming it into a spear aimed right at Naruto.

"Aaaaghhh!" Naruto hollered, losing his balance. Hisame's whip coiled tightly around his waist. Naruto wriggled and squirmed—then vanished in a puff of smoke.

"Where'd he go?" Hisame panted, looking around wildly.

"Yoo hoo! Looking for me?" Naruto snickered from the background, kicking Kirisame's back with all his might. Kirisame sailed across the landscape, slammed into a building—and instantly became liquid!

"A water clone?" Sasuke gasped.

Just then someone kicked Naruto's butt. He heard Murasame sneer as he rolled across the ground.

"Ha! Don'tcha just loooove clones?"

"This is it, blond boy," Hisame snarled. She cracked her whip at Naruto, who was trying to stand up.

"Get away from here!" Sasuke yelled, powerfully pushing him toward the lake.

"Hey! No fair!" Naruto squealed, right before he splashed in.

But Sasuke was too busy to argue. He crouched low to the ground, trying to avoid the whips.

"That won't work, my boy!" Murasame scoffed, grabbing Sasuke from behind.

"You're really starting to bug me," Sasuke muttered. He jabbed his elbow into Murasame's midsection just as Hisame's whip coiled around his wrist. Murasame doubled over in pain and retreated.

The battle quickly changed into a watery tug of war. Sasuke pulled hard on the whip, catching Hisame by surprise. She lost her balance and fell backward, right on her sorry butt again. Poor girl! Now her fancy pants were smeared with grass stains. Sasuke pinned her down and held his kunai blade against her throat.

"If you value your life, undo this jutsu," he threat-ened. Looking utterly humiliated, Hisame started to make a sign.

"That won't be necessary, Hisame," a gruff voice said.

Sasuke froze as he sensed a powerful presence behind him. Normally, Sasuke wouldn't even have flinched, but his back was completely unprotected from this new enemy.

Sasuke glanced back and saw a huge man headed his way. Strangely enough, the man was actually on the short side, but his massive waves of chakra made him look like a giant.

"Suien-san," Hisame gulped.

"What's going on here? Why are you wasting time with these youngsters?" Suien growled.

Murasame, who had been rubbing his sore stomach, sprung to his feet like a jack-in-the-box.

"Now!" he shouted at his comrades. Sasuke was jolted back to reality, but just a second too late.

"Noooo!" he gasped, as two whips coiled around his torso, one from each side. Now Sasuke was caught like a fly in a spiderweb, his arms pinned to his sides. As bad at that was, there was even more torture to come. Kirisame laughed when he saw Sasuke struggling to break free.

"This jutsu is called Rapid Thunder Whip! Wanna know

why?" he teased. Without warning, two lightning bolts crackled across each whip and brutally zapped Sasuke's body.

"Gaaah!" he cried out, writhing from the stinging shock.

"Sasuke!" Sakura shrieked, running toward him. Suddenly Suien stepped in her path. One look at his beady eyes and Sakura's knees instantly buckled under her.

"Well! Maybe we can use her, too," Suien said cheerfully. He bent over and gave Sakura a quick chop to the back of her neck. Sakura slumped forward in a stupor.

"S-Sakura!" Naruto shouted, crawling out of the water. All of a sudden he felt someone firmly pulling him back under again.

"What happened to the blond kid?" Murasame grunted. He looked at the lake, but Naruto didn't surface.

SECRET IN A BOTTLE

When Naruto finally opened his eyes, the first thing he saw was a wooden ceiling. He was lying flat on his back in what seemed to be a cave, though the floor felt nice and warm. It was quiet as a tomb, except for the faint sound of rushing water.

Where am I? How long have I been here? And why are my clothes all wet?

"Are you awake now?" asked a familiar voice. Naruto lifted his head and saw the old man Senji looking at him with concern.

In a flash, Naruto remembered everything that happened. He jumped to his feet and grimaced as pain seared down his spine.

"Don't try to move yet," Senji gently warned him.

"But...the villagers..." Naruto mumbled. "And Sakura and Sasuke..."

Senji sighed.

"Everyone has been captured, including your com-rades."

"Crap," Naruto grunted. He bit his lip and tried to stand up again. The pain was excruciating, but Naruto didn't care. Feeling like a coward hurt even worse.

"You used a lot of chakra, Naruto. Don't strain your-self," Senji pleaded, trying to make him sit down.

"I'm okay!" Naruto snapped, squirming away. Sud-denly he saw Shibuki sitting in a shadowy corner, hugging his knees. As usual, the leader of the Hidden Waterfall Vil-lage was shuddering all over.

"Why is *he* here?" Naruto growled.

"Well, um, Lord Shibuki..." Senji stammered, as Naruto marched over to Shibuki.

"Hey, you! Haven't you heard? Your village is in dan-ger!" Naruto barked at him.

Shibuki nervously darted his eyes around, unable to speak, but Senji quickly came to his rescue.

"He...he can't help it, Naruto," he said with feeling.

"Whaddaya mean he can't help it?" Naruto yelled.

"Lord Shibuki is doing his duty as village leader."

Naruto suddenly looked like he'd just swallowed a giant glob of hot wasabi.

"What are you talking about, Grandpa? He was running away from you!"

"No, no! Lord Shibuki is protecting something very important!" Senji insisted.

"More important than his villagers?"

"But he's, he's..." Senji babbled incoherently. Shibuki suddenly stood up.

"Leave Senji alone! He saved your life, you know!" he yelled. Naruto looked absolutely stunned by the news.

"Y-you dragged me into the water?" he gasped.

"Yes, I did," Senji admitted, bowing to Naruto apologetically.

"But *I* gave him the order," Shibuki said flatly.

"You!" Naruto hissed, lunging toward him. Terrified, Shibuki cowered against the wall, but Naruto got right in his face.

"So you saw the whole fight! Why didn't you help?" Naruto demanded.

"Every leader of the Hidden Waterfall has a special duty," Senji reminded him.

"What duty? Tell me!" Naruto persisted.

"N-no. That secret is passed from generation to generation. I can't—"

"Okay, okay! I'll tell you!" Shibuki cried suddenly. He signaled Naruto to follow him as he briskly walked away.

"Lord Shibuki! Please wait!" Senji pleaded, hurrying after him.

Naruto hesitated for a moment. Should he go back and save everybody? Or should he check out Shibuki's big secret?

I'm already here, Naruto figured, dashing to catch up with the others.

Soon he was climbing up a narrow, twisted passage, so steep some places were almost vertical. Naruto saw wood everywhere, and had a sudden realization.

"Hey! Are we inside that big tree in the middle of the lake?" he said with awe.

"Yes," Shibuki answered without looking back.

"What the heck's in here?" Naruto asked, looking puzzled.

"Please, Lord Shibuki! Reconsider!" Senji pleaded, desperately grabbing the back of his tunic. Shibuki roughly pulled away from him.

"Just follow me, Naruto. Okay?" he said grimly.

"Tsk! You could at least answer my question," Naruto muttered, but Shibuki pretended not to hear. When the narrow passage finally ended, they entered a small open area.

"About time!" Naruto groaned, stretching his arms. He looked around with interest. There were no lights, but it wasn't pitch black. Naruto squinted through the dim light and saw a small window.

"Here it is," Shibuki said quietly, approaching a small wooden shrine the size of a closet.

"Here what is?" Naruto asked impatiently.

Shibuki glanced at Senji. The old man shrugged in resignation. He had lost all desire to stop him now.

Shibuki opened the double wooden doors. A glass bottle dangled from a rope tied to the ceiling. It was shaped like a bottom-heavy hourglass, filled with clear liquid instead of sand.

"This is the Hero's Water," he said solemnly, holding

the bottle up to the window. The liquid glistened in the light. It was a splendid sight, but Shibuki just grimaced.

"What's Hero's Water?" Naruto asked, but Shibuki didn't answer. Finally Senji spoke.

"A secret elixir that has been passed down from generation to generation." He took a deep breath before he continued.

"The Hidden Waterfall Village is surrounded by four of the Five Great Nations. We've never had a kage, or a ninja army. But we've always been independent, even through the time of the Great Ninja War."

"Yeah, yeah, but what's all that gotta do with this?" Naruto said impatiently. He was in no mood for a history lesson right now. Senji gave him a stern look and pointed to the bottle.

"The secret to our independence is inside there."

Naruto looked dumbfounded. *Must be some wacko water jutsu,* he thought.

Senji glanced at Shibuki, who now sat on the ground, cradling the bottle in his arms like a baby.

"Every hundred years we extract a special water from this Holy Tree. One drink and any ninja instantly becomes a hero, with a hundred times more chakra at his disposal."

Where has this stuff been all my life? Naruto thought wistfully. Suddenly his eyes opened wide.

"Oh! So those guys attacked the village because—"

"Yes. They want the Hero's Water. So have many, many others. In fact, Lord Shibuki's father lost his life trying to save it."

"My father was a fool!" Shibuki suddenly burst out. "The villagers cheered him as a hero. But he knew exactly what would happen if he drank the water."

"What happened?" Naruto asked innocently. The old man looked at the ground.

"Hero's Water is a powerful weapon, but that power comes at a terrible price. The water increases a ninja's chakra, but also consumes his life force. Someone young and strong like you might survive, but most ninja perish."

Naruto looked at the bottle again and frowned. He was quickly learning that nothing about ninjutsu was as simple as it seemed.

"Do you understand now, Naruto?" Senji asked. "We must keep our villagers safe *and* keep the water away from our enemies."

"I hate this!" Shibuki sobbed.

"Sheesh. Would you quit bawlin' already?" Naruto groused. He grabbed the front of Shibuki's tunic and pulled him to his feet. Shibuki squeezed his eyes shut, but the

tears kept flowing.

"Listen up, Shibuki!" Naruto said forcefully. "I'm not exactly a genius, but I do know one thing. You can't let all the villagers die just to save this stuff!"

Shibuki opened his eyes and glared at Naruto.

"I have to protect the Hero's Water! It's my duty!" he insisted, but Naruto was still unconvinced.

"Really? Or is it just your excuse for not joining the fight?" he asked pointedly.

"You don't understand how hard it is to be village leader!" Shibuki whined.

"That's true," Naruto admitted. "I don't even wanna understand how a sissy like you must feel."

"Please stop, both of you!" Senji begged, diving between them. He gave Naruto a pleading look.

"I-it's all my fault. I told Shibuki to protect the Hero's Water…"

"You don't have to lie!" Naruto grunted. He looked so angry Senji quickly backed away. Naruto rudely jerked his thumb at Shibuki.

"This wuss came to the lake, took one look, and ran away like a little girl."

"No! I was only protecting the…" Shibuki started to say. Suddenly they heard a shout from below.

"Shibuki, Leader of the Hidden Waterfall! Are you listening?" the voice boomed.

"No! Not *him*!" Senji gasped. The voice continued.

"Your precious villagers have all been captured. Give me the water, or we'll kill them one by one."

"It *is* Suien!" Shibuki choked.

"I know you can hear me, Shibuki," Suien continued. "I used the Echo Jutsu to blast my voice all over this village. Or would you prefer to hear this?"

The next sound was a little girl screaming.

BEST MADE PLANS

On his merry way back to the Hidden Leaf, Kakashi suddenly heard a dull rumble behind him. He swung around to look and gasped with shock.

"What the—?" Was the mountain back there actually moving? Sure looked like it! Squawking birds were fleeing the area, while clouds of brown dust sullied the sky.

"Must be a landslide," Kakashi quickly figured out. "Weird, I didn't see any warning signs."

He put his ear to the ground and heard the sound of shattering rocks. Most definitely a landslide, but what should he do about it? Kakashi quickly reread his message from the Hidden Leaf.

The meeting wasn't *that* important, or the note would have arrived more furtively. A bird is plainly visible to anyone who looks at the sky. Truly important missives were always delivered by "summoning" animals, beckoned by a special jutsu that Kakashi was about to release.

He calmly jabbed his fingertip with his kunai, quickly made a sign, and pushed the bleeding finger into the ground. After a loud crackling sound, a small brown dog appeared, clad in a tiny blue vest and a Leaf headband.

"Sorry to bother you, Pakkun," Kakashi said sincerely. "Can you please tell Lord Hokage I'll be a little late?"

"Sure. Did something happen?" Pakkun drawled lazily, scratching behind his ear with his hind leg.

"Maybe," Kakashi sighed. "Let's hope it's noth—"

But before Kakashi could finish, Pakkun zoomed off like a furry rocket.

Kakashi turned back to the mountain and sighed.

"Hope this isn't as bad as it looks," he muttered.

82

Under the Holy Tree in the Hidden Waterfall stood a small building with a peaked roof. It was a Shinto shrine, the holiest place in the village. On special days, the villagers went there to pray.

Now the villagers sat near the shrine with their backs to each other, roughly tied together like bunches of flowers. Some sobbed bitterly, while others prayed in silence.

A dark red torii gate stood before the shrine: two tall posts linked together at the top by another post. A tied-up body dangled from the crosspiece, while another body was bound to the bottom of a post.

All of a sudden, the dangling figure stirred. Kirisame looked up scornfully.

"So! You finally woke up!" he scoffed.

Sasuke didn't reply. The Rapid Thunder Whip Jutsu had completely knocked him out. While Sasuke was unconscious, Kirisame had bound him with wire and hung him from the torii. Sasuke tried to wriggle free, until a sharp pain shot up his arm.

"Don't even try," Kirisame snorted. "I make that wire myself. It could slice your hands right off."

Sasuke gave him a blank look.

"S-Sasuke?" Sakura called faintly.

She sat below him, bound to the post with the same kind of wire. She looked up at Sasuke with anguish.

"All tied up and still worried about the boyfriend? How cute!" Hisame sneered, getting right in Sakura's face. Suddenly, she smiled.

"Don't you worry, honey. Kirisame will tear him to shreds later," she promised.

Sakura shuddered, but forced her lips into a crooked smile. For one surreal second, the two of them beamed at each other. Then Hisame angrily slapped Sakura's face.

"Don't get fresh, princess," she snarled.

"That's enough, Hisame," Suien grunted from behind

the torii.

Hisame bowed and quickly scurried off. She wanted to get away from Suien, and you really couldn't blame her. Pure evil seeped from every one of his pores.

Sakura sensed that evil moving toward her, but Suien passed through the torii and headed for the villagers. Sasuke also felt Suien's incredible power, but for some reason, it didn't really frighten him.

"Time to let Shibuki know we're serious," Suien told his associates.

"Yes, Suien-san," Murasame said, bowing. They were

unfailingly polite thugs, to their boss at least. Murasame raised an eyebrow at Kirisame, who instantly got the message. He plucked up a little girl by the back of her dress.

Sakura gasped. It was Shizuku from the pond, looking absolutely petrified. Sakura screamed at Kirisame without thinking first.

"Hey, you! Why pick on a little kid? You'd have more fun hurting somebody like me."

Kirisame glared at her, but he didn't drop his prey.

"Sure, if you insist! We'll definitely hurt you later! But *this* little darling is first," Kirisame leered, twisting Shizuku's tiny arm behind her back. The little girl cried in agony.

"Suien-san! Why are you doing this?" a villager begged to know, but Suien just ignored him.

"You once fought for this village with Lord Hisen!" the man persisted. Suien finally grinned.

"Yeah, I did," he admitted. "But I'm sick of that life. Time to collect my reward for all that hard work."

"But what do you mean, Suien-san?" the man wailed.

Still grinning, Suien marched over and kicked him in the stomach. The man toppled over like a little toy.

"I love this atmosphere! What fun to watch losers groaning with despair!" Suien gloated. He looked joyfully at the misery surrounding him. The villagers kept their

heads down, too terrified to make eye contact.

"Gee! I wonder when your leader will come to the rescue?" he asked innocently, scratching his goatee.

"Lord Shibuki is coming for sure!" Himatsu shouted defiantly.

"Really, little boy? Let's hope so," Suien snorted. He and his henchmen roared with laughter, but Himatsu had more to say.

"You're a good-for-nothing ninja who ran away from the village!" he yelled.

Suien stopped laughing and glared at the little boy. Dangerous waves of chakra radiated from his body, and you didn't need to know ninjutsu to see them.

"What did you say, kid?" he growled.

Himatsu violently shook his head.

"Well! Sounds like you wanna die first," Suien snapped, nodding at Kirisame. He instantly dropped Shizuku and made a beeline for Himatsu.

"W-wait!" a feeble voice cried out.

That sounds like Mr. Senji! thought Sakura with alarm. She twisted around to look. The old man tottered out with his hands behind him. Suien gave him a big smile.

"Why, it's Mr. Senji, the former head of ninja!" he said sweetly. "Nice seeing you, but where's Shibuki?"

"There's no need for Lord Shibuki to be here," Senji said quietly, pulling Hero's Water out from behind his back. Suien's eyes flashed at the glorious sight.

"Let everyone go now," Senji said firmly, but Suien kept gazing at the bottle before he finally answered.

"You could have killed me once, Senji. Getting old must be sooo scary. Is this the only stunt you know?"

"I don't care what you think," Senji muttered.

"Okay, then! Give me the water or we hurt the little boy," Suien grunted. "If he isn't enough, there's plenty more."

Suien moved toward Senji with his hands out, ready for the precious prize. The old man quickly stashed the bottle behind him again.

"Sorry, but I need a guarantee," he said firmly. "When you give me the last hostage, I'll give you the water."

"Here's another idea!" Suien cheerfully replied. "How 'bout I just kill you instead?"

Senji shuddered all over.

I hope that boy remembers our plan, he thought nervously.

They had cobbled the plan together back inside the Holy Tree. When he heard the little girl scream, Naruto's

blood quickly started to boil. He needed to get down there, but how? He ran to the little window and was trying to squeeze through it when he felt someone tugging on his jumpsuit.

"P-please wait," Senji begged.

"I can't just stand here while he tortures that little girl!" Naruto protested.

"I know. But how will you rescue everyone?"

"I dunno! I'll...I'll just beat them!" Naruto shrugged. He was rarin' to go (as usual) but a little sketchy on the details (also as usual).

Senji looked to Shibuki for help, but the young leader was still lost in his own little world. Senji sighed and turned back to Naruto.

"Shall we try a decoy strategy?" he suggested.

Naruto's face lit up. He loved decoy strategies almost as much as ramen. Senji lowered his voice to a whisper.

"Suien only wants the Hero's Water, so I'll go down and show it to him."

"Okay, then what?" Naruto hissed back.

"That should give us the opening we need. Then you can rescue your comrades and, hopefully, the villagers at the same time..."

Shibuki suddenly woke up from his daze.

"That'll never work!" he argued. "He's Suien, remember? It's useless to even try."

"How do you know that?" Naruto snapped, marching toward Shibuki. "We *have to* try, or we'll never know!"

"Please stop, Naruto!" Senji begged. He pulled Naruto back with surprising strength for a man his age.

"Why should I?" Naruto huffed.

"Before he became a rogue ninja, Suien was Lord Shibuki's sensei. Now Lord Shibuki is terrified of him."

"B-but I—" Naruto sputtered.

"Just carry out our plan, please?"

Naruto had finally agreed. Now he was perched in the Holy Tree, waiting for his big chance. Naruto carefully scanned the scene below and saw Shibuki lurking behind a giant tree root. Even from a distance, Naruto could see he was trembling all over.

"Well, at least he came out of hiding," Naruto sighed. He shifted his gaze to the enemy. Suien was slowly advancing toward Senji.

"That guy does seem dangerous," Naruto gulped. He had no worries about the henchmen, even though they'd won the last skirmish. Naruto still believed they were just about evenly matched.

But Suien was in a class all his own. Their success or

failure depended solely on his actions.

Their plan was simple enough: while Senji distracted Suien, Naruto would zip down and untie everybody. The villagers would scramble into the Holy Tree, followed by Squad Seven, who could protect them from behind. The narrow passages inside formed a convoluted maze, but the villagers knew that maze well. Even if the enemies entered, they could only fight them one at a time.

"But how will Grandpa Senji get Suien away from the others?" Naruto fretted. "He said he'd give me a signal, but Suien might grab the water first."

While Naruto worried in the tree, Suien continued his march toward Senji. The old man started to back away, but he couldn't go far. If he did, Suien would surely spot Shibuki's hiding place.

"What happened, Senji? You looked so brave a while ago! Are you up to something?" Suien said accusingly, looking around for clues. Naruto shuddered up in the tree.

Please please please don't look up here, he prayed.

Suien continued his leisurely stroll toward Senji, who had quit backing away. The old man's hesitation tipped off Suien that something was up.

"Wait a minute! Is little Shibuki back there, waiting to attack me?" Suien snorted, swiftly tossing a shuriken. It arched through the air and hit a tree root, inches away from Shibuki's face.

"Waaaaah!" Shibuki screamed in terror. He jumped out from his hiding place and ducked behind Senji. Then Shibuki did a really, really, reeeeally dumb thing—even for him.

"N-Naruto! Come down and get them!!" he yelled.

"Huh????"

"Ha! Didn't think this gutless wonder would ambush me!" Suien scoffed, looking directly up at Naruto. The two of them locked eyeballs for a second, then Naruto gritted his teeth and stood up on the branch.

"Narutooo!" Sakura screamed from below.

"Nice plan!" Suien snickered. "While Senji got my attention, the blond twerp was gonna ambush me! Too bad wimpy little Shibuki botched the whole thing."

Naruto kicked the branch and quickly made a sign. A gang of Naruto clones whirled to the ground, surrounding Suien and his henchmen. Suien hooted at the horde of Narutos with delight.

"You can make this many clones? Nice!" he laughed merrily.

"Suien-san!" Murasame yelled, coming to his defense. But Suien airily waved him away, like he didn't have a care

in the world.

"Don't worry about me, Murasame," Suien assured him. "Just guard the hostages, we don't wanna lose them."

"Y-yes, Suien-san!" Murasame stuttered, racing toward the villagers with the others.

"Back off!" the Narutos growled, blocking their way. While the henchmen gaped with their mouths wide open, a clone grabbed Shizuku away from her captor.

"Give her back!" Kirisame hissed, making a grab for the little girl. The clone jumped out of his reach, and gently set Shizuku down.

"Sister!" Himatsu shouted, dashing toward her. While the children reunited, the clones joined hands, forming a bright orange circle around the villagers. Then they grinned in unison at Suien's massively ticked-off gang.

"I *hate* this kid!" Kirisame glowered.

"Shocked, huh? I can bring you guys down, no sweat!" the Narutos chortled.

Suien had been enjoying the show, and now he giggled.

"Quite a few shadow clones, indeed. You're actually pretty good, kid."

"Are you surprised?" Naruto taunted.

"Not really," Suien shrugged. "But I *am* surprised that

you think you can get me with shadow clones."

"Huh?" Naruto stuttered. Now it was his turn to be surprised.

"There's a colossal difference between your power and my power," Suien calmly explained. "Sure, you can scare Murasame and the rest, but even a zillion clones can't touch me."

"Wh-whaaaaat?" the Narutos yelled. Their faces suddenly turned as pink as pickled ginger.

"Go ahead, come at me. I'm ready for *all* of you," Suien challenged.

The Narutos tried to step forward, but their feet seemed to be firmly glued to the ground. Suien was definitely stopping them, but how?

"Too scared, eh? Or is something wrong?" Suien sneered. He looked over at the torii, where a Naruto clone was quickly untying Sakura.

Suien threw a small pebble at them, jam packed full of his chakra. It shot through the air and hit the clone, who vanished in a puff of smoke.

"You are one smart kid," Suien admitted. "I've definitely changed my opinion of you."

"Blast!" the Narutos yelled, trying to break free. Suien turned and shouted to his henchmen.

"Buck up, you jellyfish! Get rid of 'em now!" Suien roared.

"Yes, Suien-san!" they shouted, quickly making signs. Seconds later, each one wielded a new water whip crackling with energy.

"Everybody run!" Naruto screamed at the villagers. "The shadow clones will protect you!"

Sadly, there was nothing to protect the shadow clones. Unlike sand clones, which can endure almost anything, shadow clones burst and vanish when seriously hurt. Soon there were only a few left. The henchmen looked around with satisfaction.

"Where are your shields now?" Murasame sniggered, stomping his foot on a fallen stack of Narutos. They went bye-bye in a curling wisp of smoke.

"Okay, then..." Naruto muttered.

"Then what?" Suien sneered.

"Then I'll do this!" the remaining Narutos shouted, jumping toward Suien with their fists up.

"Wooooo, you're fast! What a surprise!" Suien snorted, easily dodging the attacks that came from every direction.

He flicked away a clone with his fingers, like it was a tiny piece of fluff. The clone spun round and round and disappeared, pulling more clones along for the ride. Suien coolly flicked his fingers again. More clones bit the dust.

"B-but, b-but..." Naruto stammered, gaping at the damage.

"Like I said, kid. My power and your power are not the same," Suien said.

Just then the last clone disappeared, leaving only the real Naruto behind. Suien gave him a big grin.

"Heh! You must be the genuine article," he sniggered.

Naruto threw a kunai in desperation. Suien easily dodged away, then slammed his knee into Naruto's gut.

"Aaaaghhh!" Naruto gasped. He collapsed against Suien's knee, then suddenly vanished. Seconds later, Suien felt someone pouncing on his back.

"Hello there!" Naruto snickered. He had transformed himself into the kunai that a clone threw at Suien. When the clone disappeared, the real Naruto showed up.

It was a brilliant sneak attack. Naruto totally outwitted his opponent—or he should have. Unfortunately, the powerful punch meant for Suien didn't hit him or anyone else.

"You were close, kid," Suien admitted from behind.

Naruto tried to look back, but he felt paralyzed. Weird thing was, Suien wasn't even doing anything, but the pressure of his chakra had turned Naruto into stone. He couldn't even waggle his little finger.

"You must have loads of chakra to make that many clones," Suien said thoughtfully. "If I let you go now, you'll be big trouble later."

Without further discussion, Suien gave Naruto a mighty kick. Naruto scudded across the landscape, slammed into a tree, bounced off, and rolled right back to Suien.

He gazed down at the barely conscious Naruto, then poised his foot above Naruto's head.

"Time to die, kid," he muttered.

SUIEN SURGES ON

"Stay away, Lord Shibuki!" Senji shouted, feverishly making signs. Though his face had more wrinkles than an umeboshi plum, Senji still possessed plenty of power. As an amazing swell of chakra poured forth, a giant whirlpool swirled around his feet.

Poor Shibuki fell down in shock at the sight, then awkwardly crawled away. Senji watched him, trying not to cry, as he completed the signs for his jutsu.

"Water Style: Giant Vortex Jutsu!" he shouted.

The whirlpool that had been circling Senji became a huge tsunami—surging straight for Suien.

"Suien-san!" the henchmen screamed in horror. Suien wildly swung his head around to look.

"Giant Vortex? Crap!" he grunted. He took his foot off Naruto's head and started making signs at the speed of light.

"Water Style: Water Barrier Formation!" Suien's voice

boomed.

An invisible wall instantly surrounded him, and not a second too late. The huge tsunami crashed into the wall, but Senji's jutsu wasn't wasted.

"Waaaaah!" the henchmen screamed as the giant wave chased them down. Suien looked over and groaned. He could really care less about his cohorts, but now his prized hostages were in danger.

"Crap!" Suien grunted again.

The tsunami knocked out his henchmen and most of the villagers, though a few were still okay. Some bustled about helping their comrades, while others walloped the terrible threesome.

"Wh-what was that?" Hisame gagged, spitting out a

mouthful of muddy water. She was sprawled untidily below the torii, looking like a big wet ugly rodent.

Lucky for Squad Seven, being tied up had kept them out of harm's way. Sasuke still hung from the torii, Sakura was still bound to the post, and Naruto was still unconscious.

Suien looked back to make absolutely sure before he faced his elderly nemesis again. Senji stood in a daze, endlessly making signs, but he looked ready to keel over any minute now.

"How can some senile old geezer use the Giant Vortex?" Suien jeered. Senji suddenly grinned.

"Beats me!" he chuckled. "It just happened somehow."

Suien, however, was not amused. He stomped toward Senji and grabbed his shoulders.

"No way can an old man use a powerful jutsu like that! Did you drink the Hero's Water? Did you?"

Senji didn't answer.

"Makes sense," Suien shrugged. "That was the only way you could fight me. Too bad! Your Giant Vortex Jutsu just sucked up every drop of your chakra."

"S-Senji is in danger! Lord Shibuki, please save him!" a villager cried out.

Suien gave him a dark look. The villagers winced and

started creeping backward.

"Get away from here! Hurry!" Senji urged them.

The villagers looked puzzled at first, then nodded and jumped in the lake. Suien watched until the last one disappeared underwater, then faced Senji again.

"Feh! I don't need hostages anymore," Suien scoffed. He deftly snatched the Hero's Water away from Senji, then held up the bottle like a trophy.

"I did wonder if this was the real thing. No need to investigate now."

"Give it back!" Shibuki cried from his hiding place. Suien swung around to sneer at him.

"Shame on you, leader of the Hidden Waterfall! Even the old man's out here kicking butt! After I drink this, I'll kill you first."

Suien roughly pushed Senji away, then sensed a kunai sailing toward his back. As he swerved to miss it, another kunai clinked against the hourglass. Suien ferociously looked around for the culprit.

"I missed him!" Naruto wailed.

"Not you again! Do you have a death wish, kid?" Suien muttered, removing the cork from the bottle.

A few drops of Hero's Water dribbled out, but Suien caught them with his tongue. He took another sip and gazed blissfully at the sky, then looked over at Naruto.

"Congratulations, twerp! You're gonna be my first guinea pig!" Suien beamed. "But don't worry, your death will be totally painless!"

After that, Suien stood perfectly still, waiting for the big rush. When a few minutes went by and nothing happened, he looked down at his torso with shock.

"My chakra should be increasing! What's going on?" he snapped.

"Did you honestly think I'd bring the real thing here?" Senji said, smiling faintly.

At first, Suien looked stunned, like someone had bopped his head with a daikon radish, but his beady little eyes soon turned menacing.

101

"So this isn't real, huh?" he snarled. Naruto was surprised too.

"But, Grandpa! I thought you were—"

"Sorry, Naruto," Senji said sincerely. "I didn't trust you with a secret, so I lied. But my lie helped the villagers escape."

"If this isn't the Hero's Water, how did you release that Giant Vortex?" demanded Suien. The old man shrugged and smiled again.

"Who knows? Maybe a dying old man gets one last

chance to build up that much chakra."

Suien stared at Senji for one long moment, then knocked him to the ground with a single punch.

"This geezer tells a good joke," he muttered. Ominous waves of chakra now vibrated off his entire body. Suien reached down and grabbed Senji's long white hair and dragged him to his feet.

"Tell you what, old man. Show me the real Hero's Water, and I'll forgive you," he proposed. When Senji didn't answer, Suien tugged on his hair even harder.

"Show me! Now!!!" he screamed. Naruto had seen more than enough. He dashed up and grabbed Suien by his legs.

"Stop it! Grandpa will die!" he pleaded. Suien swatted Naruto away like a gnat and kept on glaring at Senji.

"So! Are you willing to talk now?" he growled.

"Go ahead and kill me," Senji said quietly. "You'll never find the water, even if you dig up the whole village."

Suien swung Senji around by his hair like a puppet on a string, then suddenly let go. The old man hit the ground hard, but Suien didn't bother to watch. He was too busy picking long white hairs off his jacket.

"Grandpa!" Naruto cried. He tried to go to him, but his legs wouldn't cooperate, and the grass was still slippery from Senji's tsunami.

"Now what?" he despaired.

"Naruto!" somebody hissed. Naruto glanced around but didn't see anybody.

"Up here!" the voice persisted.

Using every ounce of strength he had left, Naruto propped himself up on his elbows. Then he looked up and saw Sasuke still dangling from the torii.

"S-Sasuke? What did they—" Naruto stammered. But the sole surviving member of the Uchiha Clan was not in the mood for small talk.

"Hurry, throw me a kunai," he snapped.

"Huh?"

Naruto gaped at Sasuke, whose arms were still tightly bound next to his body. What in the world could he do with a kunai?

"Just give it to me! Do you want the old man to die?"

"O-okay," Naruto said, reaching into his pack. Sasuke caught the kunai in his mouth and started swinging his body back and forth like a pendulum.

"N-Naruto? Can you p-please help me?" Sakura called out weakly. As Naruto cut through Sakura's bonds, he heard Suien's angry voice again.

"Thought you could fool me, eh? You may be old as

dirt, but you're still a master."

Suien slammed Senji to the ground again. His body looked like old rags at this point, but Senji gazed serenely at his enemy—who immediately freaked out.

"Stop lookin' at me, old man!" Suien shrieked. He grasped what little hair Senji had left and punched him in the jaw. Shibuki shuddered as he watched from behind a tree root. Suien threw him a nasty look.

"After I beat this geezer to death, then it's your turn," he grimly promised. "I'll break one bone at a time until you finally tell me the truth."

"Wh-why are you doing this?" Shibuki stammered.

"I want power," Suien said simply. "You need power to

get ahead in this world. With the Hero's Water, I can be the best ninja around, instead of rotting away in a little village like you."

Senji suddenly felt tears in his eyes, and gave Suien a sorrowful look. He could now barely talk, but managed to wheeze out a few simple words.

"This...is...regrettable. You could have been...our best ninja."

"Thanks for the compliment, old man! But those days are over," Suien said carelessly. Senji kept looking at him with pity, making Suien extremely uncomfortable.

"Why you looking at me like that?" he barked.

"You have...changed," Senji sadly replied.

Suien raised an eyebrow.

"Yeah? How so?"

105

"You...used to polish your skills. Now you take the... easy...path."

"Do I really?" Suien said with a smile. He was still smiling as he gripped the old man around his waist.

"Die, old man!"

Senji had no strength left to resist, as Suien tossed him away like a spitwad. Right before Senji hit the ground, Naruto ducked under him to break the fall.

"You still have enough strength to do that? I *am* sur-

prised," Suien gasped.

"Just stop it, okay? If you hurt him again, he really will die," Naruto begged.

"That's the idea, brat!" Suien howled. "Get outta my way!"

Suddenly the atmosphere turned dark and very alien. Suien looked over at Naruto, who was still carrying Senji on his back. As soon as their eyes locked, every single hair on Suien's body stood up.

"No way will I get outta your way!" Naruto bellowed in a voice that sounded like thunder. Suien instantly jerked backward, like he was shoved by some spectacular force.

"Th-this can't be..." he choked, as masses of chakra surged out of Naruto. Consuming that much chakra would have killed most ninja, but Naruto seemed to have a boundless supply. And this chakra was ominous.

"Who *is* this kid?" Suien whispered to himself.

THE ONE THAT GOT AWAY

The swirls of red chakra merged together to form the head of a giant fox. Suien swooned at the sight, stabbing his kunai into his thigh to break the terrifying spell. He quickly gained control of his body again, but the creature moved closer and closer...

Suien screamed in terror as the fox opened its jaws wide. Then suddenly the beast became granular and collapsed like a washed-out sand castle. Naruto lost consciousness and slumped to the ground.

"Who is this kid?" Suien gasped again. In all his years of battle, he'd never seen anything quite like this. Suien focused his remaining chakra into his hand, then kneeled next to unconscious Naruto and raised his arm. One swift chop and the blond kid would be history...

Normally, Suien would have sensed someone behind his back, but the sight of the Nine-Tailed Fox had completely unnerved him. Suddenly he felt a cold steel blade

on the back of his neck.

"Game over," Sasuke said grimly. Suien quickly rolled away from him and leaped to the edge of the lake.

"You punk!" Suien spat out, but his beady eyes now flickered with fear.

There was no greater shame for Suien than to be conquered by a couple of kids. He had committed merciless acts for years, hoping to kill off the cowardly part of himself. But Sasuke had clearly seen Suien's weak spot—and he was about to pay dearly for that.

"I'll kill you," Suien growled, leaping backward. He landed on the lake without making a single ripple, like it was solid ground. Then he pulled out a small scroll, bit his fingertip until it bled, and blotted the blood across the paper.

"Come forth, Konenmaru!" Suien yelled, quickly making signs. He set the scroll on the water and took a deep breath.

Just then an enormous black catfish surged out of the lake, glistening in the sun. Its huge gaping mouth was set off by a pair of long spiny whiskers. Konenmaru quickly spewed a torrent of water, which Sasuke deftly managed to dodge. But Sasuke couldn't escape the whiskers, which the catfish coiled tightly around his legs.

"Blast!" Sasuke gasped, grabbing his kunai. He tried desperately to cut himself free, but the catfish shook off the blade and raised Sasuke high above the water.

Sasuke gritted his teeth, steeling himself, as Suien marched toward him. Suien went in for the kill, looking like the evil villain in a kabuki play. Then suddenly he swung around to look at the village.

Here's my chance! Sasuke thought. He quickly cut himself free, sailed across the water, and landed on the shore. Sasuke scrambled out of Suien's reach, but he really didn't have to bother. For some reason, Suien had suddenly lost all interest in him.

"We'll finish this later. I have another problem to deal with," Suien snapped.

"Running away, huh?" Sasuke sneered.

Suien glared back at him, then disappeared. Konen-maru swung its mighty tail and dove back into the lake.

When Naruto finally opened his eyes, Himatsu and Shizuku were kneeling beside his futon, looking at him with concern. Naruto quickly sat up and started barking questions at them.

"What happened? What happened to Suien?" he squawked.

"Shhh!" Shizuku hissed, pointing to a futon across the room. The old man Senji was sleeping peacefully, looking very small and frail.

"Is Grandpa okay?" Naruto asked nervously.

"Grandpa Senji is hurt real bad. He's still unconscious," Himatsu said sadly, shaking his head. Naruto looked at Senji again and sighed.

That old man risked his life for this village, he thought wistfully. Suddenly Naruto grimaced.

"What happened to Shibuki? Where is that little wimp?" he snarled.

"Don't call him that!" Himatsu protested.

"But he didn't even try to help you or Grandpa!"

"That's not true!" Himatsu still insisted.

"Is too!"

"Is not! Get out of here!" Himatsu shouted. He threw a wet towel at Naruto and burst into tears. Naruto swallowed hard. He didn't mean to make the kid cry, but how could he convince him his leader was a loser?

"I just don't get it," Naruto said softly. "Why do you all keep defending him?"

"I *said* get out! I hate you!" Himatsu sniffed.

"All right, all right," Naruto muttered, rising from the futon. He marched out into the hallway to find Sasuke leaning against a post.

"Yo," Sasuke said, looking at the floor.

"Sasuke! You're okay!" Naruto gushed.

"Of course I am," Sasuke answered sullenly. He leaned forward to whisper in Naruto's ear.

"Suien took off, by the way. But he'll probably be back."

"No problem! Next time, I'll beat him to a pulp!" Naruto vowed. Suddenly Naruto turned a little pink and nervously shuffled his feet around.

"Uh, by the way, how's Sakura?" he finally stammered.

"Come see for yourself," Sasuke grunted, heading for the door. Outside, Sakura sat on a rock in the early morning light, yawning and twiddling her thumbs.

"Sakura!" Naruto cried out with joy.

She swung around with shining eyes, but then her face quickly assumed its usual you-are-so-dumb-Naruto expression.

"Why did you have to scare me like that? I thought you really croaked this time," she snapped.

"S-sorry..." Naruto stuttered. He looked about to cry, but Sakura kept right on nagging him.

"You knew Sasuke and I were tied up! Why didn't you

rescue us first?"

"But I *did* rescue you! Remember?" Naruto pleaded.

"You just sent one of your clones, which got blown all to bits," Sakura pouted.

"But, but, that was the only thing I could do then," Naruto sputtered. He always felt so helpless when Sakura got on his case like this.

"Cut it out, you two," Sasuke grumbled. Sakura's harsh look instantly turned all soft and gooey.

"Sorry, Sasuke," she said sweetly. "It was all Naruto's fault, after all."

"Whatever. Right now, we need to cook up a new battle plan."

Naruto nodded vigorously.

"And how! We can't fight Suien the usual way, or we'll never win."

"Weren't you gonna beat him to a pulp?" Sasuke snickered. Naruto smiled sheepishly.

"Well, yeah. But I changed my mind."

"What the—? You mean Naruto now stops to think before he barges into battle?" Sasuke said with a smirk. He paused to rub his sore wrists, still dotted with angry red welts.

"Sakura and I poked around the Holy Tree," Sasuke

continued. "Some of Suien's grunts were around, but his terrible trio must be in hiding. And we still can't figure out why he took off like that."

"Maybe he got scared and ran away," Naruto suggested. Sasuke grunted.

"There was nothing to run away from. Battle-wise, he was in the lead. Geez, he had even summoned a huge catfish."

"So why did he run away?" Naruto persisted.

"I'm saying he didn't run away! He just disappeared during the fight. Something definitely got his attention."

Sakura, who had been quietly listening, now added her two yen worth.

"Maybe he sensed someone coming," she said thoughtfully. "Someone who could stop him from getting what he wants."

"How could they even get here? The road's still blocked," Naruto pointed out. Sakura shook her head.

"Someone like Kakashi-sensei would have no problem..."

The three looked toward the road with excitement. Maybe Kakashi really was on his way! Their fearless sensei would know exactly what to do with a ruthless rogue like Suien.

113

Squad Seven was right. Kakashi was on his way, albeit at a snail's pace. He had hoped to reach the Hidden Waterfall in a few hours. Now, after one whole night on the road, Kakashi dangled from a cliff, considering his next move. Destruction was everywhere he looked: knocked-out bridges, blown-up hills, tree trunks strewn here and there like chopsticks.

"They sure made one colossal mess," he sighed.

He let go of the cliff, softly landing near a guidepost they'd passed the first time around. Kakashi kicked up speed until he reached the next cliff, but the view from there really surprised him. Was that the Hidden Waterfall Village in the distance? He thoughtfully stroked his chin through his mask.

"I sure don't remember this from the first trip," he mused out loud.

Before, the village wasn't even visible until they had entered the valley. Now all the trees and ledges had been blasted away, courtesy of Suien. Just yesterday, this cliff had been a mountain.

"They should take better care of nature," Kakashi grumbled. He started running down the face of the cliff, which was almost vertical. About halfway down, Kakashi stopped, sensing something very strange. Focusing his chakra, he stuck his hands and feet to the slope, then pulled up his headband to reveal his sharingan.

Kakashi's left eye sported a bright red iris, within which floated three black *tomoe*, or comma-shaped symbols. Not only could his sharingan copy any jutsu it saw, it also came in handy when he needed especially clear vision, like right now.

Kakashi carefully scanned the landscape. What had looked like another landslide was actually much more sinister.

"They put a Maze Shield here? Guess they really *don't* wanna see me again," he muttered.

True to its name, a Maze Shield transformed even the most boring stretch of land into a complicated maze. Whoever entered the area immediately got lost, even if they previously had a good sense of direction. The jutsu itself was pretty simple, though blanketing an entire mountain with it must have taken some sweat.

115

Kakashi took his left hand off the ground and made several long, complicated signs. Then he slowly lifted his right hand, leaving his palm print in the dirt. The print glowed brightly for one split second, then faded away.

"Someone is definitely trying to trip me up here," Kakashi figured. "So I've got to get back to that village, no

matter what."

Kakashi sighed again, then took off running.

WET AND WILD

Suien had created the Maze Shield hours before, in the deep dark still of the night. After he blew up the mountain, he hammered a line of stakes into the ground, each marked with a special jutsu. Suien poured his chakra around the stakes like fertilizer, then stood back to admire his work.

"Done! This will screw up that Kakashi for a while," he said confidently. His three henchmen gazed at the Maze Shield with wonder. How could Suien create something so evil in just a few hours?

"Amazing," Murasame whispered. Suien brushed off his long gray coat and shook out his peacock-feather hair.

"I'm off to the Hidden Waterfall," he said. "But I'll be back before Kakashi shows up. Hang around here 'til then, okay?"

"Of course, Suien-san," Murasame said. The three rogue ninja of the Hidden Rain quickly kneeled before their leader and bowed their heads.

"We're just petty crooks," Murasame admitted. "But we'll never forget what you've done for us, Suien-san."

"We three will stick by you no matter what happens," Hisame pledged, placing a hand over her heart.

"Always and forever, Suien-san," Kirisame chimed in.

"Thanks for the kind words. I happily accept your gratitude," Suien said gruffly, bowing to them. Then he jumped over some shattered rocks and disappeared. A few minutes later, Suien looked back in the direction of his henchmen.

"Just try to hold back Kakashi, losers," he sniggered. "That's about all I can expect from the three of you."

Back in the village, Naruto stretched his arms out wide and gazed up at the sun. Squad Seven was still marking time outside Senji's house, waiting for Suien's next move.

"They didn't come back last night," Sasuke muttered.

"Neither did Kakashi-sensei," Sakura said sadly.

"C'mon now, Sakura! We were just guessing that Sensei might come back here!" Naruto said kindly, trying to make her feel better.

"Naruto's right. We can't depend on Sensei," Sasuke said firmly. "Who knows why Suien took off, but he'll definitely be back."

Naruto and Sakura both swallowed hard. Sasuke looked

searchingly at Naruto.

"So where is that Hero's Water?"

"Still inside the Holy Tree, I think. But it's a real mess in there. I could never find the place again."

They all looked at the massive tree.

"Then let's not even worry about the stuff," Sasuke concluded. "If we try to find it, the enemies will be right on our tails anyway."

"We should evacuate the villagers first," Sakura suggested. "If Suien comes back, he might try to take more hostages."

Naruto and Sasuke nodded in agreement.

"Grandpa says they usually hide inside the Holy Tree at times like this," Naruto said.

119

"But is that safe? This is Suien's hometown, remember?" Sakura asked worriedly.

"The villagers will be okay. That tree is humongous inside too," Naruto assured her. Suddenly he sighed and slumped his shoulders.

"What's wrong?" Sasuke asked.

"Getting into the tree is no problem. But those passageways are so twisty-turny! Only Grandpa can navigate them, but he's still in pretty bad shape."

"What about Shibuki? The village leader would surely

know the way," Sakura said practically. Naruto frowned.

"Didn't you see him shiver when Grandpa was fighting? Who knows where he—"

"I-I'll be the guide," wavered a weak voice behind them. Squad Seven swung around to look.

Senji hobbled out from his house, leaning heavily on a black cane. He had a splint on his right arm, a splint on his right leg, and a bloody turban of bandages wrapped round his head.

"Grandpa!" Naruto cried.

"I'm all right. I just took some food pills," Senji assured him. Ninja often relied on food pills to boost their chakra in desperate situations.

"You should be resting," Naruto urged, but the old man just smiled.

"I'm the only one who really knows the Holy Tree," he asserted. "It's the least I can—"

Just then Senji's face turned ashen and he coughed up a thick glob of blood. Sakura rushed to his side.

"I'll stay here and help Grandpa," she offered, gently taking Senji's arm.

"When the fight begins, I won't be able to help much," Senji warned. "Someone must protect the villagers."

"Right," Sasuke nodded, but Naruto just grumbled and

looked around.

"Where did Shibuki go?" he sputtered. Senji bowed deeply to him.

"Please don't criticize our leader," he said quietly. The other villagers seemed to agree with him, judging from the dirty looks they gave Naruto.

"Why do you keep defending him?" Naruto wailed.

"We feel sorry for Lord Shibuki," Senji patiently explained. "He may be cowardly, but he's also very kind. Besides, he never wanted to lead our village. He just inherited the post from his father."

"Yeah, yeah. He's still a big wuss," Naruto huffed.

"Please, Lord Shibuki suffers enough. That's why we leave him alone."

"But he should do his duty!" Naruto declared, clenching his fists. Sasuke quickly pulled him away.

"Let it go, Naruto."

"But, but..." Naruto sputtered.

"C'mon. We need to get ready for Suien," Sasuke said. Naruto grimaced but fell silent. Suddenly the little boy Himatsu cried out with joy.

"Lord Shibuki! You're okay!"

Shibuki shuffled onto the scene, sheepishly hanging his head. Though Senji could barely move, he limped over

to stand beside him. Shibuki completely ignored the old man and gave Squad Seven a haughty glare.

"So what are you going to do?" he snapped. Naruto gaped at him in astonishment.

"What are *we* gonna do?" he hissed, making a dive for the young leader. Sasuke quickly grabbed him from behind.

"C'mon! Just one measly little punch!" Naruto pleaded.

"No, stupid! That won't solve anything!"

"Sasuke's right! Stop it, Naruto!" Sakura admonished.

Shibuki had backed away from Naruto in fright, but now he puffed out his chest, desperately trying to look like the leader he was supposed to be.

"We will all hide inside the Holy Tree," Senji informed him. "Miss Sakura will guard us, while the other two fight the enemy."

"With no help from Shibuki," Naruto muttered under his breath. Shibuki shot him a withering look, then turned to the villagers with his head held high.

"Excellent. Then I will lead everyone to the Holy Tree," he said confidently.

The villagers cheered and clapped their hands. Naruto looked absolutely dumbfounded.

Naruto and Sasuke stood watch as Sakura and the villagers quickly boarded several boats that would ferry them to the island. Now that Shibuki was leading them, the villagers actually looked cheerful.

"Can you believe that jerk?" Naruto huffed.

"He's a real piece of work, but just forget about him. Suien is our big problem now," Sasuke muttered. Naruto looked surprised.

"Do you really think he's that good?"

"Maybe not as strong as Kakashi-sensei, but Suien is definitely jonin class. If his terrible trio show up, we'll have our hands full."

"Hoo-boy," Naruto sighed, rubbing his sore neck. Though he was pretty banged up, Naruto had amazing powers of recovery, thanks to the demon spirit sealed inside him. At any rate, he was ready to wallop Suien with everything he had, plus a little bit more.

123

The boats soon reached the island. Naruto and Sasuke watched as Senji entered the Holy Tree first, followed by the villagers, Sakura, and Shibuki.

"Now we stick around here until Suien shows up," Sasuke muttered. They moved to the middle of the village plaza and waited. And waited. And waited some more.

"We've been here for over an hour! Are they ever gonna

show up?" Naruto groused.

"Be on your guard, Naruto," Sasuke cautioned. "This waiting game could be part of their strategy."

"I know that!" Naruto whined. "But I hate just standin' around like this!"

All of a sudden, the atmosphere around them turned dark and very evil. Sasuke and Naruto instantly crouched into battle position.

"Sorry to keep you waiting, boys," a voice sneered from the lake.

Suien stood atop a tall column of water, greedily licking his lips. He quickly scanned the village, then grinned down at Naruto and Sasuke.

"So you stashed the villagers inside the Holy Tree, eh? Thanks! Now I don't have to deal with them!"

Sasuke made the first move, hurling his kunai. Suien just snorted and got out of the way.

"Tsk! You two seem even dumber than before," he clucked.

Meanwhile, Naruto had been making his signs for the Shadow Clone Jutsu. In a flash, several Naruto clones zoomed toward Suien, but he just rolled his eyes at them.

"Not those stupid shadow clones again! Is that the only jutsu you know?"

The Naruto clones threw a storm of shuriken at Suien, but he caught every spinning star and hurled them back. Two clones burst on the spot, but the others managed to get away. As Sasuke kept hurling kunai, Suien just sighed and shook his head.

"You scumbag! Quit treating us like fools!" Naruto sputtered.

"Calm down, Naruto!" Sasuke warned, seconds before Suien's counterattack blew him away. Sasuke rolled across the ground to get out of Suien's range, then quickly jumped to his feet. Meanwhile, Naruto and his remaining clones got down to business.

"Here we come!" Naruto shouted, as the yellow-haired army charged at Suien. While the fighting wasn't exactly fancy, they attacked Suien from every direction. Soon he toppled off the column of water and floated ashore.

"Tsk! You disappoint me, blond boy! What happened to all that amazing chakra of yours?" Suien scoffed.

Naruto's clones charged at him again, but Suien still expected an answer.

"No comment, huh?" he barked, lifting one hand. Inside his cupped palm was a spoonful of water. Suien added a dash of chakra, turning the liquid into a long, sharp sword.

"Water Style: Water Blade Manipulation Jutsu!" he yelled. He swung the sword samurai-style, straight through the line of clones. Most of them popped and disappeared, leaving only two stragglers behind. As Naruto and Sasuke regrouped in the background, Suien admired the damage.

"A pitiful sight indeed," he snorted. "You two have some nerve to fight me all alone. Or are there more of you?"

Suien gazed pointedly at a row of wooden barrels at the edge of the plaza. Naruto tried to seem nonchalant, but the wild look in his eyes gave him away. Suien grinned and disappeared, quickly popping up behind a barrel.

"Nice move! The real blond boy hides back here with a paper bomb!" Suien chortled. Naruto turned around with dismay.

127

"H-how did you know?" he stuttered.

"I smelled oil, dummy!" Suien scoffed. "Didja really think I'd fall for such a childish stunt?"

"Yeah!" Naruto grinned.

"Huh?" Suien gasped, as the barrels became more clones. Suien struggled and squirmed, but the clones clung to him like white on rice. Naruto threw a paper bomb into the only remaining barrel and leaped out of the way.

The barrel exploded with a roar, instantly igniting Suien's long black coat. While Suien struggled to snuff

out the flames, Sasuke gave him a swift kick right where it counted.

Suien hit the ground and started rolling around, still trying to put himself out. Sasuke and Naruto seized the opportunity to pellet him with shuriken. Youch!

"Ya dirty little punks!" Suien hissed.

Creating the Maze Shield had used up most of his chakra, slowing his reaction time down to a crawl. After a supreme effort, Suien finally managed to spread chakra all over his body, which instantly doused the flames. Then he wobbled to his feet and started to make more signs.

"Now's our chance to stop him, Naruto! He's dead tired!" Sasuke yelled.

"No problem!" Naruto yelled back, leaping in front of Suien. He quickly concentrated chakra in his arms and legs and became a punching-kicking machine. But Suien managed fend off the attacks as he continued making signs.

"Does this guy ever give up?" Naruto moaned.

Now Sasuke added his fists and feet to the fight. Suien gamely kept making signs, but it wasn't easy. Suddenly Sasuke made some signs of his own.

"Phoenix's Holy Flames Jutsu!" he shouted, spitting out a dozen small fireballs. Suien quickly caught fire again—or so they thought. On closer inspection, what had looked like Suien's body was actually a long barrel stave.

"He used the replacement jutsu!" Sasuke gasped.

"Too bad! Too late!" Suien smirked, dunking his arm in a barrel filled with water. The liquid instantly rose up to become a living, sloshing blob.

The blob of water flowed toward Naruto's kunai and hooked itself on the tip of the blade. All of a sudden the blob turned into an arm. Soon another arm appeared, followed by legs, a torso, and the crowning touch: a liquid head that looked exactly like Suien.

"I can deal with you dimwits," the water clone snickered, grabbing Naruto's elbow.

"Leggo!" Naruto cried in agony, but the clone held on tight.

"Naruto! Duck!" Sasuke shouted, as he made signs for the Fireball Jutsu.

But Suien's clone shifted shape like an amoeba and gobbled Naruto up. Now Naruto was trapped in an undulating blob of water, unable to breathe.

Sasuke turned toward the real Suien and breathed out a gust of red-hot fire. The blob of water spit out Naruto and splashed over to shield Suien. Sasuke's ferocious fireball turned the blob to steam, but when the steam dissipated, so had the enemy.

"Where'd he go?" Naruto shrieked.

"Where do you think?" Suien snickered from the background.

Naruto and Sasuke swung around. A mighty battalion of Suien water clones sped toward them, brandishing blades instead of hands.

"Repel them with your chakra!" Sasuke shouted to Naruto, but Suien's clones didn't go down easy. In fact, they just shifted their shapes and dodged every attack.

"We have to get to the real Suien!" Naruto howled. Sasuke looked over at the island and shook his head.

"This is not good," he muttered.

"Huh?"

"While we were dancing around with his clones, Suien took off for the Holy Tree," Sasuke grimaced. Naruto immediately made signs for the Shadow Clone Jutsu.

"Quick, get to the tree! I'll take care of these guys!" he shouted.

"Okay, Naruto! I'm counting on you," Sasuke said hastily, jumping into the lake. Suien's clones went after him, but they didn't get far, thanks to Naruto.

"Forget about Sasuke! You slimeballs are gonna fight me!" he shouted. More water clones showed up, and the battle began.

131

A Real Eye-Opener

After hours of picking his way through the Maze Shield, Kakashi was finally crossing the valley on the trail that followed the stream. It had been a long, exhausting trek.

"Hope the worst part is over," he muttered to himself.

"No way," a voice said from the background.

Kakashi slowly turned around. Murasame stood on a rock, leering at him. The green stripe across his nose looked as dumb as ever.

"I don't want any trouble here," Kakashi said firmly.

"Kakashi and his famous sharingan! Get ready to die, dude!" Murasame growled.

"Let's just call this a draw, shall we?" Kakashi calmly proposed. "I walk away, you walk away."

"Quit joking around, jerk!" Hisame hissed, floating down as gracefully as a rose petal.

"We have orders to stop you right here," Kirisame added, jumping out from behind a pink azalea bush.

"There's three of you? That's really weird," Kakashi said innocently, scratching his head.

"What's really weird?" Murasame snapped. Kakashi looked around with interest.

"Where are your other comrades? I clearly sensed something bigger than just you three."

"Go ahead, pal! Try and find 'em!" Murasame challenged. Maybe the great Kakashi wasn't so great after all! So what if he had a big ol' sharingan? He obviously didn't know everything.

"If you wanna fight, let's get started. I'm in a hurry," Kakashi grumbled, impatiently tapping his foot.

"Game on, big shot!" Kirisame growled, sticking his fingers into the stream. Soon he was swinging at Kakashi with a rapid thunder water whip that crackled with lightning.

"You're a little slow," Kakashi drawled.

Kirisame gaped in horror at his whip. Two kunai formed an X at the tip, effectively freezing the weapon into place. Now matter how hard Kirisame pulled, the whip wouldn't budge.

"A simple trick, really," Kakashi commented. "I put my chakra into those kunai. You'll have to undo the jutsu to free your whip."

Kirisame just glared at him, while Hisame stepped forward with another whip.

"You think you're soooo smart!" she sniveled, swinging at Kakashi's torso. Kakashi jumped straight up, missing the whip by half an inch.

Murasame came next. Kakashi easily deflected his whip with a quick flick of his kunai. Murasame sailed backward and slammed right into Kirisame, who howled with pain.

"How dare he treat us like this!" Kirisame hissed, picking himself off the ground.

Bruised, battered, but not ready to give up, Murasame leapfrogged over Kakashi and landed on the swiftly flowing stream. His skills were actually quite advanced, but taking down a jonin like Kakashi required extra effort. Murasame built up chakra, made his signs, and released his signature jutsu, the most powerful weapon in his arsenal.

135

"Water Style, Hail Barrage!" he shouted.

The water instantly froze into a dozen jagged chunks, which whizzed toward Kakashi from every direction.

"Interesting!" Kakashi exclaimed, knocking down every hail bullet with his kunai. He even hit the bullets behind him, as though he had eyes in back of his head.

But Murasame wasn't worried in the least. This was actually his master plan. Distract Kakashi at eye level, then

annihilate him from above. Murasame's eyes gleamed as one last bullet soared straight toward Kakashi's head. Sure enough, the sensei was too busy to look up.

Please don't move, Murasame silently begged. Suddenly Kakashi grinned and tilted his head. The last hail bullet hit the ground with a splat.

"That was close. Wanna try again?" Kakashi chortled.

"Crap!" Murasame groaned, kicking the ground. Meanwhile, his comrades were quickly spawning new water weapons for their next assault.

While Kirisame went at Kakashi with a water spear, Hisame flung water kunai in quick succession. Murasame also got back into the game, making signs for the Heart Acceleration Jutsu.

136

Kakashi still looked supremely relaxed, though a touch more determined. Speeding up his movements, he easily repelled Hisame's water kunai, knocked away Kirisame's water spear, and sent him flying toward Murasame. The two henchmen narrowly avoided another collision by pushing away from each other with their feet.

Now the battle went into high gear. The men grazed Kakashi's body with special water spears that grew longer or shorter on command. Hisame helped out with her water kunai, until Kakashi finally had to retreat.

"Whoa, not bad! Sorry I messed with you three. Time to get serious," he chuckled, pushing up his headband.

"The sharingan!" Hisame gasped.

"He's just bluffing!" Murasame hissed. "Let's go at him again and buy time for Suien-san."

"So your master's called Suien, huh?" Kakashi said casually, like he was chatting up a pretty girl at a cherry blossom viewing party.

"Shut up!" Murasame seethed.

Kakashi crouched down and made a quick sign, holding his right hand open at his waist. A bolt of lightning wrapped around his hand with a popping sound.

"Th-that's chakra!" Murasame gulped.

"Get out of the way," Kakashi said menacingly. Murasame's knees turned to tofu, but he still tried to look like a tough guy.

137

"Nope! I ain't movin' one inch!" he swore.

"Suit yourself. But you are in extreme danger," Kakashi warned.

Suddenly Suien's gang felt an extraordinary presence behind them. They swung around and gaped at the stream with their mouths wide open.

"Konenmaru?" they gasped in unison.

Suien's giant catfish instantly spat a torrent of water at

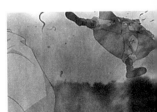

Kakashi. Strangely, he didn't even try to miss his master's henchmen. Konenmaru just didn't seem to care if they got wet, or hurt, or torn to tiny pieces.

"Agggggh!" Murasame screeched, as a killer wave smashed him against a rock. Hisame was nearly swept away, but grabbed onto a branch just in time. Kirisame managed to escape, but looked absolutely stunned.

"Konenmaru! What's going on?" he croaked.

"You three are no longer needed. I have orders to kill you along with Kakashi," the giant catfish calmly replied.

"No! Suien-san would never say that!" Murasame protested.

"Unfortunately, he did. Suien hid that huge catfish before he left you," Kakashi said quietly. He had dodged the raging current by jumping backward.

"No!" Hisame screamed.

"Suien-san told me to kill you all," Konenmaru repeated in a dull voice.

"Not if I can help it, catfish!" Kakashi suddenly yelled, dashing forward. Konenmaru furiously whipped around his whiskers, but Kakashi was way too fast for him.

He grabbed his right wrist and started focusing chakra in his palm. Suddenly his hand made a violent crackling sound, like a thousand birds chirping at the same time.

This was Chidori, Kakashi's killer attack, a swift and powerful assassination jutsu. Kakashi had once used the Chidori Jutsu to saw a lightning bolt right in half.

A ninja's body must be supremely tempered to focus so much chakra into a single spot. And since Chidori is a head-on attack, the user needs excellent eyesight too. In fact, the only two known masters of the technique both possessed the sharingan.

Konenmaru kept on spitting water, but the Chidori Jutsu had turned the bone-crushing torrent into a harmless little trickle. The last thing the catfish saw before going under was Kakashi's glowing hand.

Suien was touching down near the Holy Tree when he suddenly clutched his chest.

"Konenmaru...is dead," he choked. "And Kakashi is on his way..."

Suien was definitely not ready for him. Setting up the Maze Shield had consumed lots of chakra, while the battle with Naruto and Sasuke had used even more. Even worse, losing the powerful Konenmaru was like losing his right arm. For Suien, it was now or never time.

"C'mon, Shibuki! Show me the Hero's Water!" he shrieked, looking around like a fiend. Suddenly he detected a slight movement inside the Holy Tree's massive trunk.

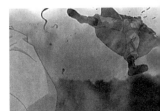

Suien furrowed his thin eyebrows and focused hard. His efforts were soon rewarded when he spotted someone peering at him from inside. Suien cheerfully waved at them.

"Why, hello there! Who are you?" he sneered. His beady eyes glittered as he started walking toward the tree.

TWO BOYS AND A BAD GUY

After the villagers had been safely installed near the Hero's Water shrine, Shibuki plopped on the floor, looking like he'd just beaten the heck out of somebody—and lost.

"Are you all right, Lord Shibuki?" the children's mother asked in a worried tone.

"Yeah," Shibuki answered dully. He retreated into his own little world again, until he noticed Himatsu scampering up to the skylight to peek outside.

"Don't climb up there! What if the enemy sees you?" Shibuki scolded harshly. Himatsu looked stricken and quickly came down, then hid behind his mother.

"I'm s-s-sorry, Lord Shibuki," he whimpered. Shibuki kept glaring at the little boy, until he noticed the villagers were looking at him uncomfortably.

"What?" Shibuki snapped at them.

"Everyone feels anxious, Lord Shibuki. Please say something to reassure them," Senji kindly requested. Shi-

buki darted his eyes in the other direction.

"Please, Lord Shibuki," Senji pleaded. Shibuki buried his face in his arms.

Meanwhile, the clone vs. clone bout was still going strong. Naruto's clones bravely fought on, until a really weird thing happened. All of a sudden, every Suien clone vanished from the battlefield.

"Where'd they go?" Naruto gasped, cautiously looking around. He stood on guard for a moment, but Suien's clones didn't return. As Naruto shut down his own clones, he suddenly had a harrowing thought.

Did Suien find the Hero's Water?

Naruto quickly glanced over at the island. Suien was nowhere to be seen. Suddenly Naruto saw a flash of light near the roots of the Holy Tree. Was that chakra?

"Hoo-boy! This looks really bad!" he groaned, jumping into the water. He crossed the lake with swift strokes, huffing and puffing all the way.

Sasuke, who had already reached the island, now crept carefully toward the Holy Tree. He didn't sense anything ominous, but Suien was a master of surprise and probably an expert at Hiding Jutsu.

Should I go in and look around? Sasuke wondered. But if

the Holy Tree was as complicated as Naruto claimed, why even bother? Suddenly Sasuke felt a really strong tingle down his spine.

"Boy, you kids are cunning! That really ticks me off!" a familiar voice snapped.

Sasuke slowly turned around. Suien glowered back at him with murder in his eyes, his body glowing with chakra.

He's so strong again! What happened? Sasuke thought frantically.

Just a little while ago, Suien had seemed completely spent. But Sasuke figured this second wind probably wouldn't last all that long. Candles always glow brightest just before they burn out.

"Showtime," Sasuke muttered, opening his eyes wide. Almost instantly, his irises both turned crimson, while three black comma-shaped tomoe appeared within them.

"You...have the sharingan too?" Suien choked. No wonder the kid was so good! He had a Kekkei Genkai, a special trait passed down to him by his ancestors. Suien should be so lucky!

Sasuke boosted his chakra until it exploded, then buzzed toward the enemy, who stood still as a statue. Hurling a kunai as a distraction, Sasuke attacked Suien's blind spot even faster than before.

Suien quickly covered his body with chakra-infused water, which deflected Sasuke's attacks like a sturdy suit of armor. But Sasuke easily saw through the new jutsu, and tried to confuse Suien with some phony attacks. Using the extra speed from his sharingan, Sasuke pretended to go for Suien's stomach, then quickly kicked him in the butt. Poor Suien spun around like a top, never knowing which body part was about to get pummeled.

He quickly ran out of steam, unable to deal with Sasuke's increased speed. Every attack left him with another bump,

bruise, or bloody nose. Sasuke sensed the time had come to finish Suien off.

"Good-bye, Suien!" he yelled, attacking him from behind. Suien sailed across the landscape and crashed into the Holy Tree headfirst. Then he hit the ground and stopped moving.

Is he really dead? Sasuke wondered, looking over from a safe distance.

Suien's chest heaved slightly, so he was still kicking. Sasuke dashed over and shoved a kunai under his throat. Suien listlessly raised his head.

"This isn't over yet," he muttered.

"Huh?"

All of a sudden Sasuke felt a chill. He looked down to see a stream of muddy water slithering up his legs.

"Nice trick, huh?" Suien gloated. "Every time you came at me, I passed on some of my water armor! I just pretended to be fooled by your fake attacks!"

Sasuke desperately tried to repel the jutsu, but the water stuck to his body like glue. The liquid kept rising until it completely covered his head.

"Noooo! Not my eyes!" Sasuke shrieked.

"Good thing you're still a young pup," Suien smirked. "If you really knew how to use that sharingan, you woulda seen right through me! Now you can't see at all!"

Suien slowly rose to his feet, then jammed his knee into Sasuke's ribcage. Poor blind Sasuke didn't even see him coming. As Sasuke fell backward, Suien savagely punched his skull.

"You two brats are full of surprises! One kid with a chakra monster, the other with the legendary sharingan!"

Sasuke felt ready to vomit, but he quickly wiped his eyes and glared up at Suien.

"Quit lookin' at me like that!" Suien snarled, kicking Sasuke's stomach again. Sasuke started to gag.

"I know where the Hero's Water is!" Suien sang out. "It's just so darn obvious..."

He concentrated his chakra in his legs, looked up, and kicked the ground. But just as he was flying into the air, a loud voice boomed at him from behind.

"I'm Naruto Uzumaki! Here to kick your butt!"

Naruto jumped out of a tall column of water, dashed forward, and kicked Suien with all his might. Suien hit the Holy Tree with a loud thunk, then slid down the knobby trunk on his bare hands, landing on a giant tree root. Suien looked up and saw Naruto—and giggled like a silly schoolgirl.

"Hee hee! So it's you again, kid!"

"Yep, it's me!" Naruto growled, bashing his fist into Suien's gut. Blood spurted from Suien's mouth, but he just hugged his sore stomach and tottered to his feet.

"Nice job, blond boy," he muttered.

Naruto was helping Sasuke get up, but he took time out for a little brag-fest.

"No kidding! I'm gonna be the Hokage of the Hidden Leaf some day! I'll clobber a runt like you in jig time!"

"So Suien-san is a runt, huh? Go ahead, try to beat me!" Suien challenged, sticking out his right arm. A water sword slowly emerged from his hand.

"You don't have to give me permission, scumbag! Here I come!" Naruto bellowed.

To Suien's surprise, Naruto proved to be a formidable opponent. Battling Suien and his gang had definitely taught him a thing or two. When Sasuke finally got the mud out of his eyes, he couldn't believe how fast—and how tough—his teammate had suddenly become.

What Naruto lacked in form he made up for with sheer power. Suien gasped for breath and kept on swinging the water sword. Though Naruto was riddled with injuries, he still managed to drive his enemy into a corner.

Suien gasped and wheezed as his water sword quickly lost its shape. While Suien hurriedly tried to rework the blade, Naruto seized the moment.

"Yaaaaaaaaah!" he yelled, slamming another fist filled with chakra into Suien's solar plexus.

"Gaaaagh!" Suien choked, spitting out even more blood. The sword dripped away from his hand like an icicle melting in the sun. Suien opened his mouth wide and tried to suck in more oxygen, then suddenly crumpled to the ground.

"How's that?" Naruto cried triumphantly, doing a little victory dance.

"Not yet, Naruto! Watch out!" Sasuke shouted from the background.

"S-say what?" Naruto sputtered.

Too late! Several water vines swirled up from the ground, wrapping around Naruto from his ankles to his chin.

"Wh-what is this stuff?" Naruto cried, furiously squirming inside the liquid cocoon.

"Water Style! Transform-at-Will!" Suien snickered.

He was still sprawled on the ground, but the fight was far from over. While Naruto was celebrating his big win, Suien had gathered up bits of his broken sword and pumped them full of chakra, turning the water into vines. It seemed like a brilliant move—but even evil masterminds

149

screw up sometimes.

"Blast it!" Suien suddenly snapped. He grabbed on to a nearby rock and struggled to pull himself up. When he finally got to his feet, he glared over at Naruto.

"That jutsu should have strangled you to death. I must be losing my touch," Suien muttered, diving into his pocket for some food pills. He stuffed his mouth full and ground them between his teeth.

"Stay right where you are," he told Naruto. "After I drink the Hero's Water, you're the first victim on my list." Suien took a few deep, measured breaths, then closed his eyes and concentrated.

"No, I'm not!" Naruto shouted, throwing his kunai. It soared straight toward Suien's cold black heart, but he caught it just before it pierced his coat.

"That was way too close. I really have lost it," he sighed, tossing the kunai aside.

Naruto and Sasuke looked stunned. Was this really the end of the day? Unfortunately, no such luck. Suien closed his eyes again and started making signs. Suddenly he opened his eyes wide, kicked the Holy Tree's trunk, and flew up.

"Where is he going?" Naruto blurted from his liquid prison.

"To get the Hero's Water," Sasuke muttered.

"Not if I can help it!" Naruto vowed. But no matter how much he wriggled and squirmed, the water vines held fast.

A THIRST FOR POWER

Inside the Holy Tree, a woman screamed and pointed above her head. The villagers looked up to see Suien sneering down from the skylight.

"Yippee! The gang's all here!" he said cheerfully, wriggling through the window like a big snake. He slid down the wall on his back until his feet hit the floor.

"Shibuuuuki! Where are you?" he sang out as the terrified villagers huddled together.

"Aw, never mind. Is the Hero's Water in there?" Suien asked, jerking his thumb at the wooden shrine. Nobody said anything, but Suien didn't really expect an answer. He swaggered toward the double doors, where Sakura nervously stood guard.

"Stop right there!" she warned, brandishing her kunai.

"Such a brave little ninja girl! Just don't get carried away, honey."

"Why not?" Sakura snapped, stepping forward.

Suien instantly coiled his arm around her neck and lifted her off the ground. Sakura started to choke, but Suien just snorted. Suddenly he tossed Sakura away like an apple core and gleefully opened the double doors.

To Suien's complete and utter shock, the shrine was empty inside.

"Bad news, people! Your leader cares more about the Hero's Water than his villagers," he said darkly. Then he swung around and grabbed a pretty young woman by her long black hair.

"Do you know where Shibuki is?" he demanded.

"No!" she said defiantly.

"Yeah, right!" Suien snarled, hurling her against the wall. The whole tree shuddered. The woman fell to the floor, still alive but badly injured. Suien restlessly paced around, sweat dripping down his forehead.

"Better get out here, Shibuki! Your dear villagers are getting hurt! C'mon, show your face!"

Sakura watched him from nearby, worrying about what to do. She could finally breathe normally, but her body still ached all over.

They keep on protecting Shibuki, Sakura thought sadly. *But why?*

The young leader had left with the Hero's Water just

minutes before Suien showed up. The villagers had looked puzzled, but no one dared to speak up.

"S-stop it! Let mama go!" a tiny voice suddenly shrieked.

Sakura instantly snapped out of her reverie and looked over at Suien. He had the children's mother in a choke hold, while Himatsu and Shizuku punched his legs with their tiny fists.

"Nooo!" Sakura shrieked. She tried to stand up, but a stabbing pain in her collarbone brought Sakura to her knees. Suien angrily shoved the mother away and plucked up Shizuku by her tiny arm.

"All the little children just love you, Shibuki!" he sneered. "I'll kill one kid at a time 'til you show up!"

Shizuku felt the cold blade of Suien's kunai under her chin. She opened her mouth to scream, but nothing came out.

"Sasuke...Naruto..." Sakura moaned. There was nothing else she could do.

Shibuki wandered aimlessly inside the tree until he reached an opening that led outside. Too tired to go any further, he sat down and leaned against the doorway. He crossed his arms against his chest, protecting the Hero's

Water still stashed beneath his tunic.

Why can't they just leave me alone? he thought for the zillionth time. The wistful looks the villagers gave him made Shibuki feel like a total flop. He stared into space for what seemed like hours until someone called his name.

"Shibuki! What the heck are you doin' here?"

Shibuki quickly glanced up. Naruto dangled from a branch like a macaque monkey, while Sasuke stood scowling behind him.

"N-Naruto?"

"Why aren't you with the villagers?" Naruto demanded to know.

"Um, well, I..." Shibuki stammered, stalling for time.

Naruto jumped and landed right in front of him. Shibuki quickly looked away, but Naruto knelt down and shook him by his shoulders.

"Listen up, you! Suien knows where the water is!"

Shibuki's eyes nearly popped out at the shocking news.

"N-no!" he croaked.

"Everybody's in danger now! We have to go rescue them!" Naruto insisted, pulling on Shibuki's arm. The young leader refused to budge and sadly shook his head.

"Now what's wrong?" Naruto grumbled. He was getting really tired of Shibuki's lame excuses.

"The Hero's Water is right here," Shibuki said, pointing to his chest. "When Suien finds out the shrine is empty, he'll leave them alone and come looking for me."

"Are you crazy? What if he holds all the villagers hostage again?"

Shibuki turned away and squeezed his eyes shut.

"Just leave him alone, Naruto," Sasuke sighed.

Naruto glowered and walked away. Suddenly they heard Suien again, his jeering voice amplified by the Echo Jutsu.

"Come back, Shibuki! Before even more blood gets spilled!"

Naruto and Sasuke glared up at the Holy Tree.

"C'mon, Naruto. Let's not waste any more time here," Sasuke grunted, leaping to a higher branch.

"Right!" Naruto agreed, bending his legs to jump.

"Why can't they just leave me alone?" Shibuki whined. Naruto looked down at him and sighed.

"What do you mean?" he asked quietly.

"I'm no hero. I just succeeded my father," Shibuki muttered, staring straight ahead. He pulled the Hero's Water from his tunic and continued.

"My father was no hero, either. He was just a fool."

"You can't really mean that!" Naruto protested. "Your dad was a great guy!"

"Yeah? How would you know?" Shibuki retorted, rising to his feet. While Shibuki silently fumed, Naruto brushed back his hair and re-tied his Leaf headband.

"Only a hero would sacrifice his life to protect his village," he finally muttered. Then he jumped onto the nearest branch.

Looking dazed, Shibuki watched Naruto leap from limb to limb until he disappeared from view. Soon Suien bellowed again, only this time he was ready to bargain.

"I'm gonna count to ten, Shibuki! Bring me the bottle, or I rip this sweetie to shreds! Ten!"

"Don't listen to him, Lord Shibuki!" Shizuku cried. "He's a bad, bad man!"

"Nine!" Suien yelled. "My, what a noble little girl. Noble little girls make me wanna puke." He twisted Shizuku's tiny arm again, making her scream for mercy.

"S-stop it! My sister will die!" Himatsu pleaded, digging his fingernails into Suien's ankles. Suien kicked him across the room like a soccer ball. Sakura reached out and grabbed the little boy right before he hit the wall.

"Eight!" Suien barked. "Show yourself, Shibuki—or your little darlings really will die!"

"Stop it!" someone yelled from above. Sakura looked up and gasped.

"N-Naruto?"

159

Squad Seven's most unpredictable member leaned through the skylight, sweating like a sumo wrestler.

"So my jutsu finally wore off, eh?" Suien grinned. "I'm kinda busy right now, but hang around! I'd just looooove to fight you two again!"

Suddenly Suien grinned at the wooden shrine.

"Come out and join us, sharingan boy! I know you're back there!"

Sasuke angrily stepped out from behind the shrine, while Naruto jumped down from the skylight. Suien ignored

them both and continued his chilling countdown.

"Seven! Six! Five!"

Shibuki still didn't answer.

"Four, three, two, one, zero!" Suien said in a rush. "Congratulations, Shibuki! The little brat croaks!"

Suien swung his kunai at the back of Shizuku's small neck, right between her pigtails. All of a sudden the little girl vanished, replaced by a feisty kid in a orange jumpsuit.

The kunai meant for Shizuku pierced Naruto's back instead. Naruto pushed the little girl to safety before he slumped painfully to the ground.

"Well! You're full of surprises, blond boy," Suien snarled. He grabbed onto Naruto's hair, dragged him to his feet, then suddenly tossed him away like an old shoe.

"You really irk me, punk! Why do you have to keep butting in?" Suien snapped.

Now Naruto was face down, the kunai still lodged between his shoulder blades. Every breath he took felt absolutely excruciating.

"Naruto!" Sasuke yelled. Suien gave him a ferocious look.

"I've planted more of my famous water vines in here," he huffed. "Take one more step, and the villagers will get squeezed to death."

"I'm...I'm okay, Sasuke," Naruto croaked. "G-go save the others..."

"Awww! Look at the little hero!" Suien taunted. "Let's see just how much you can really endure."

The villagers shuddered as Naruto screamed in agony. Before her mother could stop her, Shizuku dashed forward and grabbed Naruto's hand.

"Stop hurting him!" she shouted at Suien. Himatsu quickly ran to protect his sister.

"Out of the way, brats!" Suien screeched. "I just kept you alive to lure out Shibuki, but I'd dearly love to bump you both off!"

"You don't scare us! We have Lord Shibuki!" Himatsu said bravely. Suien threw back his head and laughed like it was the funniest joke he'd ever heard.

"Shibuki the coward? He ditched you guys, remember?"

"That's not true!" Shizuku insisted.

"Lord Shibuki is our hero!" her brother chimed in.

"I don't have time for this!" Suien snarled, sweeping them both away with one swing of his arm.

"Wait," a voice said quietly from the background.

Suien looked up. Shibuki stood across the room, star-

161

ing at the hourglass-shaped bottle in his hands.

"About time you showed up!" Suien beamed. "Didn't you hear me calling you? Hand over the Hero's Water right now."

Shibuki kept gaping at the bottle, trying to make up his mind. All of a sudden he looked up, then slowly headed for Suien.

"Hold on, Shibuki! What are you doing?" Sasuke called out to him.

"Giving him the Hero's Water," Shibuki muttered, and kept on walking.

"But, but how could you?" Sasuke asked desperately.

"What else can I do?" Shibuki shrugged. In his mind, this was definitely a lose-lose situation. If Shibuki didn't hand over the Hero's Water, Suien would surely kill the villagers. But once Suien drank the water, he'd probably kill them all anyway. Shibuki paused near Sasuke and patted his shoulder.

"It's okay. I'll figure out something," Shibuki assured him. Then he raised his head high and took the last few fatal steps.

"Finally! Fork it over!" Suien ordered, holding out both hands.

"Not until you let everyone go," Shibuki said firmly.

Suien raised his eyebrows. Had wimpy Shibuki suddenly grown a spine?

"What happened? You're like a whole different person," Suien scoffed, but Shibuki didn't back down.

"Well? Will you release them?"

"Gimme the water first. I don't wanna be duped by another fake," Suien snarled.

Shibuki shook up the bottle and smiled.

"Don't worry. This is the real thing," he whispered.

"Good. Put it right here," Suien said, greedily wiggling his fingers.

"Promise me, Suien. Promise you won't kill anyone."

Suien grinned, then stretched out both of his arms and

bowed dramatically to his former student.

"Sure! We used to be master and disciple, after all. I've gotta respect a request like that."

Shibuki took a deep breath and held out the bottle. Suien quickly grabbed it, almost swooning in ecstasy.

This is it! he thought, holding the bottle up to the light. As everyone watched in horror, Suien removed the cork and took one delicious, glorious sip.

Suddenly Shibuki noticed Naruto was lying at his feet. He leaned down and gave Naruto a rueful smile.

"You're a fool just like my father," Shibuki sighed, shaking his head. For once in his life, the blond kid didn't know what to say.

SOMETHING REALLY FISHY

"Hah! This *is* the genuine article! The real Hero's Water!" Suien exclaimed, re-corking the bottle.

Almost instantly, his body started to inflate like a big balloon. His chakra shot out fiercely, making every hair on his body stand up. Suien thrust out his arm—which was softly glowing—and grabbed Shibuki by his throat.

"Farewell, my friend. But don't worry, you'll have company in the afterworld. Every single villager will be going along for the ride!"

"You made a promise, Suien!" Shibuki shrieked.

"Did I? My memory is just so darn feeble nowadays," Suien mocked, tightening his grip. Suddenly Suien felt a strong hand on his wrist.

"Whaddaya think you're doing?" he growled.

"This, Suien," Shibuki said calmly, as his arm slowly grew bigger.

"N-no way! D-did you—?" Suien sputtered.

"Yep! I drank the Hero's Water too!" Shibuki exclaimed. "Now I'm gonna rip *you* to shreds!"

Shibuki knocked Suien's hands away from his throat and hurled him through the skylight. Suien soared to the lake, followed by his former student.

Just as Suien gently landed on the water, Shibuki dived straight for his head. Unfortunately, the rogue ninja still had quite a few tricks stuffed up his sleeve.

"Water Style: Giant Waves!" Suien suddenly hollered.

The water instantly swelled up into giant waves that crashed toward Shibuki. But he quickly shielded himself with his chakra, tossing the waves right back at Suien.

While Suien easily repelled the water with his hands, Shibuki started making signs at a breakneck pace. He soon finished and placed both palms on the surface of the water.

166

"Water Shadow Blade!" he yelled.

Giant waves as sharp as razors rolled toward Suien, but he just snorted and put his palms on the lake. The water instantly cascaded upward, forming a sturdy wall that blocked Shibuki's jutsu.

"You can't win, Shibuki! I taught you everything you know, remember?" Suien hollered.

"I've grown up, Suien!" Shibuki hollered back, landing

right in front of his foe. "I'm not that timid little boy who used to worship you."

"*Pfft!* Do you want to die that badly?" Suien sniggered.

"Let's just fight and see what happens," Shibuki shrugged.

"You have some nerve, scum!"

Shibuki and Suien jumped up at exactly the same time, scattering their chakra around like confetti. Soon towering columns of water popped up all over the lake.

Squad Seven anxiously watched the battle from the base of the Holy Tree. Injured Naruto leaned on Sasuke for support as they cheered Shibuki on.

"Just look at the power of the Hero's Water," Sasuke gasped, pointing at the lake.

167

"What a fight," Naruto whispered in awe. Behind them, Sakura nervously chewed her fingernails.

"But whoever drinks that water could die, right?" she asked earnestly.

"It completely sucks out a person's potential chakra," Sasuke admitted. "Only the strong survive."

Suddenly Naruto felt uneasy.

"Do you think Shibuki will be okay?" he asked in a small voice.

So far, the fight looked about equal. But Suien's peer-

less jutsu soon took over, forcing Shibuki to defend himself. He easily fended off Suien's attacks at first, but then his energy started to fade.

Suien, on the other hand, looked fresh as a lotus blossom. Years of training had taught him how to make the most of his chakra. Shibuki had plenty of power but not much experience, and soon ran out of options.

I'll die if he keeps this up, Shibuki thought, pausing to catch his breath. Suien seemed to read his thoughts and quickly stepped forward.

"I've trained hard for this moment, while you grew up as a coddled boy. Simply put, I'm still better than you."

He attacked Shibuki again with terrifying speed. Shibuki managed to get away, but his face looked as white as the snow on Mount Fuji.

"There's no way you can win! I know every jutsu that you do!" Suien bragged.

Shibuki stared at Suien, frantically trying to remember his old lessons. Suddenly he pulled out a scroll, bit his finger until it bled, and smeared a dark red line across the paper.

"You're wrong, Suien! There's one jutsu you don't know!" Shibuki crowed, rapidly making signs. He placed the scroll on the water's surface and opened his mouth to yell.

"Ryurimaru, come forth!"

A huge crimson and white koi leaped out of the water, the same fish Shibuki's father had summoned six months before. Shibuki jumped on Ryurimaru's back, but Suien was far from impressed.

"Big deal! I can summon something way bigger than that puny little minnow!" he bragged, pulling out his own summoning contract. He smeared the scroll with blood and threw it on the lake. Seconds later, a giant black catfish appeared, even larger than Ryurimaru.

"My name is Rainenmaru!" the catfish said. "Did you summon me?"

"I'm your new master! Obey me!" Suien said gruffly, jumping on its back. The catfish dove underwater.

"Careful, Shibuki! They're looking for a chance to attack!" Ryurimaru warned.

Suddenly the huge catfish rose up right in front of them, swinging its long whiskers. Ryurimaru gracefully dodged the assault while Shibuki made more signs.

"Dragon God Transform!" he finally shouted.

Like déjà vu all over again, the giant koi became a golden dragon. It wrapped its body around the catfish and squeezed tight. Rainenmaru's bones started to creak...

Then all of a sudden, the catfish grazed the dragon with its whiskers. After a blinding flash, the dragon let go, spurted out some black smoke—and became a fish again.

Suien jumped on the dying koi, which was now floating belly-up. Shibuki just gaped at his old teacher.

"Let's end this," Suien growled, punching Shibuki's face. Shibuki sailed across the lake, landing with a thud in the village plaza. Suien sailed after him.

"Playing fishy with you was fun! Please accept this little token of my gratitude," Suien snickered, holding out his hand.

A thin wire of water flowed out and jabbed through Shibuki's shoulder like a metal spike. He screamed and writhed in agony.

171

"Good! You still can feel pain!" Suien snorted, jabbing the other shoulder. Shibuki screamed again.

"S-stop it! You've already won!" Naruto pleaded desperately from the Holy Tree. Suien just shrugged and pierced Shibuki's left thigh.

"I can't watch this!" Sakura cried, covering her face with her hands. Sasuke kept silent, but his fists were clenched into tight balls.

"Is there nothing we can do?" Naruto wailed, looking around frantically. They needed to get to the other shore—

but how?

"Please help my master," a voice suddenly said.

Naruto looked around with surprise. Ryurimaru floated at the edge of the lake, its fins tattered and torn like old rags.

"You're still alive?" Naruto gasped.

"Yes. I don't have much chakra left, but I can still ferry you to the other side."

"That's enough! We'd like you to do that," Sasuke said quickly.

Ryurimaru slowly paddled around and offered its back to Naruto and Sasuke. Just then Rainenmaru came charging at them.

"You should be dead, Ryurimaru!" the catfish roared. The koi quickly realized its number was about to be up.

"I won't have time to carry you there. Hop onto my back fin," Ryurimaru said hastily. Naruto and Sasuke stepped on its huge tail, both wondering what the big fish had in mind.

"Here you go!" Ryurimaru suddenly yelled. He flipped up his tail, catapulting Naruto and Sasuke right across the lake. They looked back gratefully, just in time to see the catfish slam into the doomed koi.

"Ryurimaru!" Naruto cried. The koi's huge body split

open, then vanished in a cloud of smoke. Shibuki burst into tears.

"Not Ryurimaru!" he sobbed. Suien smiled callously as he pierced Shibuki's right hand.

"I can't believe you're bawling over a big fish! A summoning animal is just a tool, dummy! That's why you'll never be a first-class ninja."

Suddenly Suien heard two loud thunks behind him. He turned around to see a pair of dark figures emerging from a cloud of dust.

"What did you just say?" Naruto growled, stepping forward.

"Huh? I can't hear you!" Suien lied, cupping his hand around his ear.

173

"Tell me what you said!" Naruto demanded, stomping his foot.

"I *said* he's a stupid fool! That fish was a weapon, not a pet! We never shed tears for our shuriken, do we?"

"What are you talking about?" Naruto yelled.

"A ninja believes only in himself. Anything else—or anyone else, for that matter—is simply a tool to be used."

"Do you really believe that?" Naruto hissed.

"Yep! Don't you?" Suien smirked.

"Naruto! Get away from the water!" Sasuke yelled sud-

denly.

"Wh-what?" Naruto sputtered, whirling toward the lake.

An enormous whisker appeared, swinging back and forth like a whip. Sasuke had sensed it coming and got away, but poor Naruto was just a second too late.

"Narutooooo!" Sasuke yelled, as the huge catfish knocked his teammate into the water.

"You crushed him! Good job, Rainenmaru!" Suien cheered, but then his beady eyes suddenly went blank.

"...R-Rainenmaru?"

The catfish let out an agonized howl as a tremendous force lifted its body.

"You again!" Suien gasped.

Naruto stood on the surface of the lake, holding Rainenmaru up by his whiskers. Red flames of chakra radiated from his entire body as Naruto hoisted the huge fish to his shoulders.

"No! Don't!" Suien pleaded.

Two seconds later, Rainenmaru was flying right toward him. Suien screamed and ducked, but the catfish still skimmed across the top of his head.

Rainenmaru slammed through six houses, three trees, and the local ramen joint. Finally it slid to a stop, still alive but barely breathing.

"F-forgive me, master," Rainenmaru pleaded.

"You useless piece of crap! You shamed me!" Suien roared. He quickly packed a water ball full of chakra and flung it at the wheezing catfish.

A huge explosion erupted. When the dust finally settled, all that was left of Rainenmaru was a heap of humongous fish scales.

"You got what you deserved, catfish!" Suien snarled, twirling around. Naruto was still radiating swirls of red chakra, his face contorted with rage.

"Y-you're still here?" Suien squeaked like a mouse.

"So you treated him like a tool," Naruto muttered. Suien stepped backward, not taking his eyes off the blond-haired kid.

175

"I'll never forgive you for that!" Naruto hollered, dashing forward so fast Suien couldn't even see him. Soon Suien felt a supercharged punch to his paunch. He pinwheeled through the air, then fell smack into the fish scales, which were starting to stink up the place.

"He's a m-monster..." Suien shuddered. He started to crawl away, until Sasuke sidled up next to him.

"You're not going anywhere, scumbag," Sasuke muttered. Suien tried to dodge Sasuke's kunai, but the blade

ripped right through his bicep.

What's happening to me? Suien thought desperately.

Just minutes ago, his body had felt light as a feather. Now he was dead weight, unable to even wriggle his big toe.

"Looks like the Hero's Water finally wore off," Sasuke calmly observed.

"@#$%^&!" Suien snapped. Using every ounce of chakra he had left, Suien jumped backward and took out the Hero's Water.

"I just didn't drink enough of this stuff!" he snarled, pulling out the cork. He tilted his head back and took a big swig. Seconds later, another amazing amount of chakra burst forth.

"Check it out! I can still beat you brats!" Suien gloated.

"It's over," someone said, so calmly it gave Suien goose bumps. He turned to see Naruto coolly gazing at him.

Where did he come from? I didn't even sense him! Suien thought wildly.

"You're the worst kind of scum, Suien. You believe only in yourself," Naruto muttered, bashing his fist deep into Suien's gut.

Suien gagged and fell backward. He gamely tried to get

up, but his chakra was finally kaput.

"Uh-oh! Looks like you just ran out of juice," Sasuke said innocently.

"It c-can't be over already!" Suien panted, trying to catch his breath.

Suddenly a tiny bit of chakra burst forth from deep inside Suien's body. Suien howled with glee and used this last erg of energy to run away from Naruto and Sasuke.

"Guess what, kiddies? I still have a little more Hero's Water!" he crowed.

Suien opened the bottle again and chugged down every last, luscious drop. Almost instantly, his heartbeat went into overdrive, while his body grew even bigger. More streams of chakra flowed out and madly swirled around him.

Suddenly Suien looked victorious. He flung the empty bottle on the ground and soared up into the sky. Naruto and Sasuke had to shut their eyes at the sight of so much chakra. When they finally dared to look again, Suien was still airborne, but something seemed very wrong with him.

"Look at me, boys! I'm a hero!" Suien bragged.

Those were his last words.

All of a sudden, Suien started to shrink like someone had popped him with a pin. His chakra hissed and crackled

and threw off bright blue sparks.

Seconds later, the chakra exploded with a deafening roar. Suien's body blew away like a leaf in the wind—and disappeared.

Soon a shriveled-up something dropped below the waterfall, where Kakashi stood with the terrible trio.

"What's that?" Kakashi wondered, as the thing floated to the edge of the pond. He reached out to pull it ashore—and gaped in amazement.

"It's...it's you," the thing muttered. Kakashi did a double take. What had looked like a dead fish was actually a human body!

"I'm Kakashi of Hidden Leaf. And you are?"

"Su-Suien."

His henchmen all gasped. Kakashi glanced back at them.

"Is this your master?" he whispered.

Murasame staggered forward to make sure, then quickly turned away. Hisame and Kirisame couldn't even bear to look at their old leader.

"Looks like my crew managed pretty well," Kakashi said proudly. The others, however, were in no mood to congratulate him.

"This can't be true," Murasame whimpered.

"How could we be duped by scum like him?" Hisame wailed.

Kirisame covered his face with his hands and blubbered like a little baby.

Suddenly Suien let out a low moan—and passed away.

These thugs got what they deserved, Kakashi thought, though he did feel a tiny bit sorry for them.

EPILOGUE

Shibuki survived in the end, though he had been beaten pretty badly. Thankfully, he was young enough to withstand the deadly effects of the Hero's Water. Senji also lived on, despite all he'd been through.

"Guess my long lost ninja training served me well," the old man chuckled.

After Kakashi checked in with Squad Seven, he paid the young leader a visit. Shibuki looked earnest as they discussed the events of the past few days.

"So Suien died," Shibuki said quietly.

"Yup. I witnessed his demise with my own eyes," Kakashi assured him. "A truly gruesome sight. Was that the usual side effect of the Hero's Water?"

Shibuki shook his head.

"Not really. Suien drank way too much of it."

"I see. But now that the Hero's Water is gone, how will you protect the village?" Kakashi asked gravely. Shibuki

just grinned at him.

"Actually, this could be a good thing," he said brightly. "The Hero's Water saved our village in the past, but your students showed me something even better..."

Kakashi didn't comment, but he was smiling broadly behind his mask.

A few days later, Kakashi and Squad Seven were finally ready to go home. A crowd of villagers gathered around the Holy Tree to see them off, including the children and their grateful mother. Shibuki shyly hovered in the background, until Sakura quietly approached him.

"Are you really okay now?" she asked with concern.

Shibuki nodded.

"I'll definitely have to lay off ninjutsu for a while. But I drank the Hero's Water—and survived!"

"Lucky you!" Naruto said with enthusiasm. He started to turn away, but Shibuki gently tugged on his sleeve. The young leader hesitated a moment, then finally spoke.

"Uh, Naruto? I'm...sorry about everything."

"Huh?"

"I acted like a total jerk," Shibuki said sadly. "I really made trouble for you guys."

Naruto grinned and heartily slapped Shibuki's back.

"Relax! If you weren't around, we might have all ended up dead! Besides, you're a real hero now."

"I am?" Shibuki gasped.

"Sure! You risked your life for your village, just like your father."

"Thank you, Naruto. I really appreciate that," Shibuki said sincerely, extending his right hand. Naruto shook it, looking a little embarrassed.

"See you later?" Shibuki asked softly.

"Yeah. See ya later."

Kakashi and his crew took one last look at the waterfall, then headed for the trail. They had been hiking for a good long while when suddenly the sensei stopped and

turned around.

"Uh, by the way, we may have a teensy little problem getting back to Hidden Leaf," he said evasively.

"Now what?" Sasuke groaned.

"The road's completely gone from here on out."

"But what does that mean, Sensei?" Sakura wailed.

"It means Suien and his gang destroyed the bridge and just about everything else."

"Those dirty dogs!" Naruto growled, kicking up a giant dust cloud. Kakashi settled him down and continued.

"Just consider this extra training, crew. Gotta bulk up those muscles, right?"

"Wrong!" they whined in unison. Kakashi pointed at a high cliff in the near distance.

"We'll start out easy, okay? The angle of that slope over there is only eighty-five degrees..."

"Man, this is gonna be boring," Naruto muttered.

They all sighed and started walking.